To Chris Poore,
A great friend and journalist

Reunion of Familiar Strangers

Michael Embry
10/29/22

Michael Embry

A Wings ePress, Inc.
Boomer Lit Novel

Wings
Press, Inc.

Wings ePress, Inc.

Edited by: Jeanne Smith
Copy Edited by: Christie Kraemer
Executive Editor: Jeanne Smith
Cover Artist: Trisha FitzGerald-Jung
Images from: Pexels/Pixabay

Wings ePress Books
www.wingsepress.com

Copyright © 2021 by:Michael Embry
ISBN 978-1-61309-518-8

Published In the United States Of America

Wings ePress Inc.
3000 N. Rock Road
Newton, KS 67114

What They Are Saying About

Reunion of Familiar Strangers

I've been looking forward to John Ross' 50th high school reunion since Michael Embry teased us with the possibility earlier in his Boomer Lit series.

Placing someone who is "coming of old age" in the same place he initially "came of age" is a brilliant backdrop for a story. Even better when you consider Embry has written successfully for both the Young Adult and Boomer genres. His is a voice to be trusted.

Given the antics of John's former classmates early in the reunion, it appears the old adage is true: the more things change, the more they stay the same. Never mind the transition to old age; you wonder if some successfully moved to adulthood in the first place. However, as events progress, the overly simplistic perspective that ruled the high school halls starts to fade.

Then the old class bully turns the clock back and shows a renewed interest in John's affairs. How should he respond? Is the indirect, non-confrontational approach he followed for most of his high school career still appropriate after all these years? Or should he confront him like he did that last time?

If you think the answer is obvious, keep reading, because a surprise at the end suggests it may be more complicated than that.

—Chris Boucher, author, *Pivot series*

In his latest John Ross Boom-Lit novel, *Reunion of Familiar Strangers,* Michael Embry proves once again that you truly can't go home again, certainly not to your 50th high school reunion. At least not without encountering school bullies who've never grown up, racial and homophobic prejudices, aging classmates, and your own mortality. A novel sure to bring back memories to every baby-boomer.

Nicely imagined, full of characters who will long linger in the reader's mind, and a gentle reminder that we truly can't go home again, *Reunion of Familiar Strangers* is another winner from the pen of Boomer-Lit king, Michael Embry. Don't miss it!

—Chris Helvey, Editor-in-Chief, *Trajectory Journal*

Dedication

This novel is dedicated to:

Richard G. Wilson,
longtime friend, great newspaper reporter, avid reader

and to

the class of 1966 at Eastern High School in Middletown, Ky.,
and Taylor County High School in Campbellsville, Ky.

~ * ~

In Memory of

Jeffrey G. Kerr (1950-2020)
Cynthiana, Ky.

Linda Green Morgan (1950-2020)
Somerset, Ky.

Kenneth Rappoport (1935-2020)
Old Bridge, N.J.

Jill Lynn Spaulding (1948-2021)
Fresno, Calif.

One

John Ross didn't wake up in the best of moods. He'd had a restless night, getting up twice to go to the bathroom, and once to take an antacid pill to calm the heartburn in his chest. He knew better than to eat a spicy pizza in the evening. Finally, as four-thirty-three flared on the alarm clock, he decided to get out of bed for good. He gazed at Sally, a faint glow on her soft and restful face from the moonlight filtering through the sheer beige curtains. John thought about moving over and pecking her cheek but decided against intruding on her serene slumber. He looked at her for several seconds, noticing a slight smile on her lips, almost luring him back for a kiss. He wondered if she were dreaming, and if so, what it could be about.

John barely breathed as he eased out of bed, fearing he would stir Sally from her tranquil state. He slipped his feet into slippers, put on lounging pants at the foot of the bed, and tiptoed out of the room, closing the door gently behind him. After starting a pot of coffee, he turned around to find Whiskers at his feet, eager for a few soothing strokes across his furry black back before going outside for his morning constitutional.

John stood on the front porch while Whiskers ran to the side of the house to do his thing, part of his morning routine. It was too early for the paper to arrive. He scanned the neighbors' houses. A dog howled in the distance. Moments later, another dog responded. And then another. He noticed a black-and-white cat moving stealthily about the foundation of the house across the street, perhaps following the scent of a field mouse or other small animal. Porchlights and lampposts intruded on the tranquil darkness, but that would be changing in the next hour as folks prepared for work, school, or whatever activities they had planned for the day. Whiskers took his time returning to the porch, sniffing the tires on Sally's SUV, and leaving a mark on a mulberry bush. When they went back to the cozy confines of the house, the coffee was about finished as the earthy aroma wafted in the kitchen. John put water and dry food in his pooch's bowls.

John sat at the bar with his coffee while Whiskers devoured his breakfast and then scampered back to his cushioned pad in the dark den. John picked up a manila envelope that contained several sheets he and Sally had perused before going to bed. He paused a few seconds before dropping it back on the bar. He took a sip from his coffee and shook his head. The contents were the reason for his fitful sleep.

John's stomach churned a bit. He took another swallow of coffee. He wished the paper would arrive so there would be something to take his mind off the envelope. He contemplated going downstairs to the den and watching one of the news channels, but didn't want to disturb Geraldine, his mother-in-law, who had taken up permanent residence while recovering from a hip fracture. She was a light sleeper and often shared coffee with him at sunrise, but this morning was different. The clock on the wall showed five o'clock.

In a few hours, his brother- and sister-in-law, Wendell and Libby, would be arriving to spend a long weekend with Geraldine. It wasn't the perfect solution, because Geraldine had insisted she was perfectly capable of taking care of herself, even though she was approaching her ninetieth birthday in a few weeks. Sally had to remind her mother several times that it was only a precaution in case she needed some kind of medical assistance. Geraldine didn't like that, taking umbrage that she was incapable of looking out for herself. Truth be known, she simply didn't care to spend time with Libby. She put up with Wendell only because he was her son. But they all tolerated each other for the sake of family coexistence.

There was a natural friction between Geraldine and Libby. Maybe it was Geraldine's caustic attitude about most things; maybe it was Libby's holier-than-thou demeanor. It was probably a combination of the two and more. Poor Wendell was stuck in the middle, trying to mind his "Mama" and protect his wife from her sarcastic barbs. And no doubt, save himself from Geraldine's digs. John and Sally had grown used to Geraldine's pointed opinions, although Sally would attest they were hurtful at times. John learned to dish it back teasingly. Geraldine relished the give-and-take she had with him. And he did, too, for the most part, unless she got under his skin. There was no denying she could do that—to anyone at any time and any place.

John heard a thump on the front porch. The newspaper had arrived, a rare occasion it landed by the front door. Most mornings he searched for the paper on the driveway, under shrubs, or near the front sidewalk. He stepped out and picked it up, a skeleton of what the paper had been when he was sports editor, only a year ago when he retired. The loss of advertising, mostly due to the Internet, had taken its toll on daily newspapers across the country. The only ones that appeared to be thriving were the weeklies, which didn't face the same kind of competition for advertising dollars. But John knew their day of reckoning was coming as the face of communications was ever-changing in the twenty-first century.

John refilled his coffee and opened the thin newspaper, skimming the front-page headlines before flipping over to the obituaries. To his relief, he didn't recognize any names or accompanying photos of the recently deceased. It wasn't until he had reached his early sixties that reading the obits were part of his daily routine. That's when friends, neighbors, associates, colleagues, and others began to pass on. From his time at the newspaper, first as a sportswriter and then as sports editor, he had come to know quite a few people, including coaches, athletes, celebrities, and others associated with sports.

Engrossed in a feature story about nineteenth-century iron furnaces in eastern Kentucky, John felt a soft touch on his shoulder. He turned his head, greeted by a peck on the cheek, and smiled. Sally squeezed gently, then sauntered to the counter for coffee.

John folded the paper and set it aside. "I thought you'd sleep in for another hour or so."

She sat across from him, slowly stirring a spoonful of creamer into her steaming cup. "It was tempting, but since you weren't in bed, I decided to get up. I felt a little guilty, knowing we've got a busy day ahead of us."

"Don't remind me," he said, pursing his lips for a few seconds. "This is a day I haven't been looking forward to. For a long time."

She reached over and touched the top of his hand. "I know, honey. But you're making things worse. Just try to relax."

"It's all Chloe's fault." John was referring to his soon-to-be forty-year-old daughter who lived in New York. He couldn't suppress a slight smile. "I can't believe she did this to me."

Sally glanced at the envelope at the end of the bar. "Blame her all you want, but she did it because she loves you."

"I know, but I still don't have to like it. She could have asked me first. I've got better things to do with my life."

"What things? Walking Whiskers to the park? Meeting your old buddies at McDonald's several times a week? Admit it, John, you don't have a whole lot going on these days."

"Isn't that what retirement is supposed to be? I would have found another job if I wanted to continue working."

"John, you always commented about people sitting around in rocking chairs, watching TV all day or doing things you considered mundane. You said that'd never happen to you."

"And your point, sweetheart?"

"To be honest, you're doing the same thing you've wailed against all these years. You need to find some hobbies or interests. I think you'd be much happier and content."

"Who says I'm not happy and content? I maybe enjoy doing nothing. Can't a man unwind after working for practically a lifetime? I'm in transition." He grinned.

"I think your grace period is over. Other than our trip to Budapest, you haven't done much of anything. Admit it."

He held up his hands as if signaling a truce. "You're not being fair. You know there's been some extenuating circumstances in the interim. Have you forgotten our son Brody's drug problems? Your mother's fractured hip? Chloe's cancer? The extended visit from Wendell and Libby and all that entailed? And there's been more than that, if you'd like for me to make a list."

"Touché. But maybe having an outside interest would take your mind off things. You need to be more proactive about what you want to do instead of reacting to what is going on around you."

"And what do you suggest I do?"

"Remember when you played tennis?"

"Yeah, but my tennis buddy blew out his knees."

"Can't you find someone else to play?"

"It seems like everyone else has bum knees."

"I don't think you've tried hard enough."

"Sweetheart, I'll try to do that after things settle down some more. It always seems there's one thing after another. This retirement thing hasn't gone as smoothly as I wanted it to."

"You know what they call it, don't you?"

"What?"

"Life."

"Funny, funny," he said with a twisted grin. "I would have never figured that out. You can be so insightful."

"Now you're being sarcastic, just like Mother."

A tapping on the floor caused them to turn toward the dining room. Geraldine approached in her pink bathrobe and matching fuzzy slippers, her steel-tipped cane pattering the hardwood floor.

"Did someone call my name?" she asked, sidling up to the bar.

"Mornin', Geraldine," John said as he eased off his chair. "Let me get you some coffee."

"Mother, we're just talking about events since John retired," Sally said. "It's hard to believe it's been that long."

"Seems like forever to me," Geraldine said, sitting erect on the stool.

"A blessing for you," John said, as he set a cup of coffee in front of her.

"If that's what you want to think," she said. "It's more the other way around."

"I feel that every day when I see you," John said with a wide grin. "You must feel the same when you see me."

"Are you trying to be a smart aleck?"

"Wendell and Libby should be here in couple hours," Sally said, changing the course of the conversation.

"Don't remind me." Geraldine sipped on her coffee.

"Anything you would like for me to pick up at the grocery?" John asked.

"I don't care. Make sure you get some sweets for Libby. And don't forget, she likes diet soda."

John laughed. "And butter-pecan ice cream."

"Chocolate for me."

"Ditto!"

"I still don't know why they're coming here. I can take care of myself and your little mutt perfectly well. I don't need any help."

"I've told you, Mother," Sally said with a somber expression. "In case there's a medical emergency. What if you fell again?"

"I know how to use a phone to call someone," Geraldine said, before taking a deep breath.

"I know you do, but it could be serious. And don't you want to spend quality time with Wendell and Libby? They'll keep you company."

"If you say so." Geraldine glanced at the ceiling.

"Maybe Brody will stop by to check on you," John said.

"You really think that? When was the last time he was here for more than twenty minutes?"

"He's been busy with work and rehab," Sally said. "Give him time."

"You're always giving him excuses."

"You have to when someone is making progress in rehab. Isn't that what you want?"

"Of course it is, Sally. You know that."

"Everything'll be fine. We'll be back Monday afternoon."

"Maybe earlier," John said.

Sally picked up the envelope and removed the contents.

John grimaced. "You didn't have to do that."

She held up the cover sheet and smiled. It read "Welcome to the Riley High School 50th Class Reunion."

Two

Wendell and Libby were expected at the house by ten in the morning. They arrived a few minutes before noon, even though they lived several houses down the street where they conducted a non-denominational Christian ministry. They had become involved with a Christian One group while visiting Geraldine several months earlier. The congregation, led by a spirited Sister Cathy, was busted for various and sundry un-Christian activities that included porch thefts and assorted hate crimes. Wendell and Libby were not implicated in the criminal actions. When the group dispersed, a few to jail, and others to parts unknown, Wendell and Libby moved into the house to carry on their so-called *God's work* in the community.

John answered when they rang the doorbell. They didn't exactly apologize for being late, other than to say they had got called into some more of *God's work*. John figured, after having lived with them for a few months, they had simply overslept. They used that phrase quite a bit to fend off questions or criticism. Libby's eyes were puffy, and Wendell's somnolent face had stubble. They both asked if there was anything left for breakfast.

"I did pick up a dozen long johns when I went to the supermarket this morning, thinking you'd be here around ten," John said. "I don't think Geraldine ate all of them."

Libby led the way to the kitchen, her nose picking up the scent of the pastries like a hungry dog seeking treats as she went directly to the box on the counter. It was only after she opened it that she acknowledged Sally and Geraldine sitting at the bar.

"It sure took you long enough," Geraldine said, raising her brows.

"We had some of God's work this morning," Libby said, taking a long john from the box and sitting down. "Any coffee left?"

"I'll make a fresh pot," Sally said. "It'll only take a few minutes."

"Libby knows how to make it," Geraldine said. "You and John need to be leaving if you're going to make it to the reunion on time."

Libby gave Sally a pettish stare, but the expression eased when Sally rose from the stool and prepared the coffee. Libby took a nibble from the long john...a tiny smile emerged on her pudgy face, then a big bite that brought an expression of pure ecstasy as she closed her eyes in a dream-like state for a few moments. Geraldine watched in amazement before turning to Sally and letting out a snort.

Before sitting next to Libby, Wendell gave Geraldine a peck on the cheek.

"How are you feeling today, Mama?" he asked pleasantly.

"About good as could be expected at my age."

"It's sure better than the alternative."

"What's that supposed to mean?" she said sharply.

"Uh, that you could be sick and bedridden. That's all I meant, Mama."

"Or dead!"

"Now Mama, don't say those things."

"Well, it's the truth. I'm not going to be around forever."

"Thank God," Libby mumbled to herself.

"What did you say?" Geraldine's eyes focused like lasers on her daughter-in-law.

"Uh, I was thanking God that we have you in our lives," Libby stammered with a twisted mouth. "We are so blessed. Right, Wendell?"

"I pray to God every night that we have you, Mama," Wendell said in an obsequious tone that brought a cringe from John. Sally tried to suppress a cough in the kitchen that drew attention from the others. She reached for a glass of water. "I think I got something caught in my throat." She coughed several times before sipping from the glass.

"It's true, Mama," Wendell said.

Geraldine reached into the box and snatched another long john. "Whatever."

"John, I bet you're excited about seeing all your old classmates," Libby said brightly. "I'll be having my reunion in six years, the Lord willing."

Standing with his hands planted at the end of the bar, John said, "I can't say I'm looking forward to it, but that's okay. You know this is Chloe's idea. She RSVPed and paid all the expenses as a gift for me. I only wish she'd asked me first."

"Now, John, if she had done that, you would have said no," Sally said as she carried cups of coffee to the bar for Wendell and Libby.

"Exactly," John said, his lips pressed tightly to prevent words he might regret uttering.

"It was a surprise for you."

"And that it was."

"Libby, I've made a copy of important phone numbers and put them on the refrigerator if you need to reach us for any reason," Sally said. "Of course, we'll have our cellphones."

"Did you have a big graduating class, John?" Libby asked as she reached for another long john while eyeing Geraldine as if to see her reaction.

"Maybe a couple hundred or so students in my class. The school closed a few years after I left and was consolidated with another city school in Columbus. Riley High School is no more."

"That's so sad," Libby said. "A part of your history."

"Why did they do it?" Geraldine asked. "That seems strange to me."

"Probably to improve the overall education for students, but also to cut costs," John said. "I suppose it's cheaper to have one large school than to have two smaller ones."

"It's always money," Wendell declared. "That's a shame."

"Doesn't it take money to run that little ministry of yours?" Geraldine asked.

"But that's not the same thing," Wendell said. "We're trying to reach out and spread God's word."

"If you say so. I think you'd be better off if you and Libby would just find regular jobs instead of mooching off others."

"That's a horrible thing to say," Libby cried, dropping her half-eaten long john on a napkin. "We don't mooch off anybody. We simply take donations."

"Same thing," Geraldine said, crossing her thin arms across her chest.

"We'll be rewarded in heaven someday for our work," Libby said, pushing out her ample chest. "I mean God's work."

Geraldine gave her a dismissive look. "You better hope so."

Wendell and Libby glanced around the room, their mouths agape and eyes open wide as if hoping John or Sally would rescue them from the verbal attack.

"Well, folks, Sally and I better load up the car and hit the road in a few minutes," John said, changing the subject to their disappointment.

"Do you want us to sleep in your bed?" Libby asked meekly.

"Uh, I suppose you can," Sally said. "Let me change the sheets before we leave."

"Sally, you let Libby do that," Geraldine barked.

"Mother, it's not a problem."

"That's right. It's not a problem for Libby."

"I can do it, Sally." Libby averted looking at Geraldine.

"I really don't know why they need to spend the weekend here," Geraldine said as if Wendell and Libby weren't in the room. "They only live a few houses down the street."

"Don't you want our company, Mama?" Wendell asked, his lower lip protruding like a wounded child.

"I can take care of myself."

"I know you can," Sally said. "But in case there is an emergency of some sort. Let's not take any chances. Okay? It'll make me feel better while we're away."

"Oh, if you say so," Geraldine said as she got off the stool. "I'm going to watch TV. Let me know when you leave." She scowled at Wendell and Libby and left the room.

"Sally, we've got a few minutes, so I'm going to take a quick walk with Whiskers," John said. The frisky pooch heard his name and scampered to the front door.

"I thought you were in a hurry to leave," Wendell said, glancing at his watch.

"We won't be gone long, unless you want to take him out."

"No, you go on, John. Whispers would rather be with you."

"It's Whiskers."

"I keep forgetting."

"I know," John said as he fastened the leash on Whiskers. They stepped on the front porch. A harsh sun beat down on them as they headed down the street toward the park. With the muggy heat, John didn't expect much enthusiasm from Whiskers for the walk.

Whiskers' tongue drooped as he breathed heavily after three blocks. John felt sweat beads trickling down his neck. He swooped Whiskers into his arms, turned around and carried him back toward the house. He had walked a few more doors down when he noticed Bert Reliford, his longtime neighbor, cutting grass along the driveway with an electric trimmer.

"You don't think it's too hot to be out here doing that?" John asked.

"You gotta stay on top of things or they get out of hand," Bert said, removing his sweat-drenched cap. His face was flushed.

"Mind if I say something?"

"Go for it, buddy."

"Go back in the house and let Wilma pour you some iced tea or lemonade, or whatever," John said. "It's too hot to be out working in the yard."

"You make me feel like an old man."

"We're both getting to be old men," John said with a light chuckle. "We've got to look out for each other. Especially since we both have ticker problems."

Bert drew a deep breath and wiped his forearm across his brow. "I suppose you're right."

"Go back into your house and relax with the air conditioning."

"I think I'll finish this little strip," Bert said as he pointed to the edge of driveway. "It'll only take a minute or so."

"Let it wait until it cools off later this afternoon, if you know what's good for you."

Bert gazed at John for a moment. "Okay." Without saying another word, he turned and headed to his house, clutching the trimmer.

"Stay cool," John said as he walked away.

Wendell had already loaded the luggage in the back of Sally's SUV when John returned home. Libby and Sally were in the bedroom, changing the sheets on the bed. Wendell was at the bar, chomping on another long john. Geraldine was engaged in a soap opera.

Whiskers lapped water from his bowl while John poured himself a glass of ice water and sat at the bar. His daily routine usually included a short nap and he felt like taking one now.

"Did you buy anymore long johns?" Wendell asked. "There's only one left. Or do you have any breakfast items?"

"We've got eggs, cereal, and a few other things," John said. "You should know where everything's at."

"I may have to run to the bakery in the morning," Wendell said. "You know how Mama and Libby love their pastries." He took another bite from the long john, licking the side of his mouth for a clump of the creamy filling.

"If I had time, I'd make another run, but Sally and I need to be leaving soon."

"I wasn't suggesting that. I was just sayin' how they like those sweets."

"You've got that right."

"And Mama likes pizza as well. Any of those in the fridge?"

"Uh, I don't believe so."

Wendell frowned. "Oh."

"I'll give you a twenty to order a pizza later on," John said. "We don't want Mama to starve."

Wendell's face brightened like a child about to receive a gift. "That'll be our surprise for her."

"Our surprise?"

"You know what I mean."

"I think I do," John said, lifting his brows before taking a long swallow of water.

"Anything Libby and I should know? Will Brody drop by?"

"You know Brody," John said. "He comes and goes at all times of the day. I'll send him a text and let him know you're here."

"That'd be great."

Sally and Libby walked in. "Are you about ready to leave?" Sally asked.

"I think so," John said. "It's going to be a long, hot drive."

"The weatherman said it's supposed to be around ninety-five today," Libby said. "So you guys be careful. Hear?"

Geraldine sauntered to the dining area. "Let me know when you get there."

"We'll do that," Sally said. "Just make sure your phone is charged and turned on. Unless you want us to call the regular number."

"You can let Wendell know," she said. "He can tell me."

"Be sure and take care of Whiskers," John said as he kneeled and patted the top of the dog's head.

"I may even take Whispers for a walk," Wendell said.

"It's Whiskers," John corrected, slightly shaking his head.

"Oh, yeah." Wendell nodded. "We'll go out after it cools down."

"That'd be a miracle," Geraldine said.

"Now, Mama, that's not nice. I love to walk."

"Back and forth to the refrigerator."

"I think we'd better be going," Sally said, kissing Geraldine on the cheek.

"We'll see you guys on Monday," John said. "If not sooner."

"It'll be Monday," Sally corrected, giving John a stern look.

As they stepped out on the front porch, Wendell whispered in John's ear, "Did you forget something?"

John's brows furrowed. "What?"

"Pizza money."

John forced a smile, removed a twenty and a ten from his wallet and handed it discreetly to Wendell. "That should cover another pizza if you guys get hungry."

"John, did you say you went to the grocery this morning?" Libby asked.

"I picked up a few things to tide everybody through the weekend."

"I was wondering if you got some diet soda. You know I like diet."

John palmed his hand against his forehead. "Oops. I knew there was something I forgot."

Libby's shoulders slumped.

"I'll run out and get you some later, sweetie," Wendell said. "We also need some more long johns. Right, Mama?"

"Why are you asking me?' Geraldine scowled. She shook her head and returned to the den.

John and Sally hurried to the SUV, waving before they got inside. He turned the ignition while she cranked up the air conditioner. They glanced back at Wendell and Libby standing on the porch and smiled.

"Let's get the hell out of Dodge," John said as he backed out of the driveway.

Three

When they reached Interstate 75, John set the SUV on cruise control and turned on the radio to his usual oldies station. Bachman-Turner Overdrive's "Roll on Down the Highway" boomed heavy bass lines from the overworked speakers before John turned down the volume. John and Sally hadn't talked since leaving home as she fiddled with her smartphone while John navigated the congested afternoon roads leading out of Lexington. He wasn't one to talk when there was a lot of traffic, and she knew better than to distract him, especially with idle conversation.

"I hope it's smooth sailing the rest of the way," he said, breaking their silence. "Other than being hot, the weather should cooperate. I didn't see any rain in the forecast, although it would be nice to cool things down a bit."

"I got a text from Chloe wishing us a good time," Sally said, holding out the phone. "She says to take plenty of photos."

"Photos of what? A bunch of aging baby boomers? She wouldn't know any of them."

"I think she's just interested in seeing photos of you with your friends."

"I hate to disappoint her, but I forgot my camera."

"Oh, John, how could you do that?" Sally said, creasing her brows. "Remember when you did the same thing when we went to Budapest?"

"And I had to buy a new one while we there. I don't plan to do it again in Columbus."

"We used our smartphones to take pictures. We can do that at the reunion."

"Only you would remember to do that," he said, giving her a disconcerting glance.

"I remembered something else."

"What would that be?"

Sally opened her oversized handbag and held up the small point-and-shoot camera he had purchased in Hungary. "I remembered our camera." She gave him an inflated smile.

John sighed. "Why doesn't that surprise me?"

"Don't worry, I'll take the photos of you and your old buddies and girlfriends. It'll be fun."

"I think you're going to be disappointed, sweetie. I was voted most unpopular person in the class, ugliest senior, and the person least likely to succeed. It was a clean sweep."

Sally laughed. "We'll find out this weekend, silly man. I think there's a lot you haven't told me about your teen-aged years. To be honest, I hardly know anything about your life before we met in college."

"I could say the same about you," he said. "Other than what your mother has told me, there's not much I know about you. But I'll find out when we go to *your* reunion."

"There's not much to know about me."

"Let me determine that," John said with a sly grin. "This curious mind wants to know."

"I'll be doing the same about you," she said. "I'm so excited."

"I will say it's nice to get out of the house for a few days. We've been cooped up for so long, it seems. I get stir crazy."

"I know what you mean. Ever since my short trip to see Chloe after her cancer treatments, I've been home most of the time, other than my book club. We need to get out more."

"Maybe take some day trips to towns around the state. Did I ever tell you about that old gal I met from Madisonville on my flight back from New York?"

"I don't remember."

"She was a retired teacher and a widow. I believe her name was Alma. I'd like to pay a surprise visit to see her."

"How old was she?"

"A few years younger than you," John said, keeping his eyes on the road.

"Oh, really? Now I know why you want to go there."

"Honey, she was probably in her eighties. I just wanted to get your reaction."

"You got me on that one," she said. "But I do like your idea about going on trips. Maybe we could take Mother along with us."

"That's fine with me. She's mentioned a few times how she'd like to get out of the house once in a while."

"I've offered to take her with me to places around town, but she always makes excuses for not going. Usually, it's some favorite program on TV. I also think she's not as strong since fracturing her hip. She seems to tire more easily."

"We'll both work on her," John said.

"Brody seems to be busy with his work and rehab."

"Let's keep our fingers crossed that everything is going well. I'd hate to have another emergency call about an overdose this weekend."

"Let's not even go there. I think he's doing well. I'm proud of him."

"Don't you think that us attending support classes bolstered his confidence?" John asked.

"You never know with him. But I'd like to believe he appreciates our concern."

"His girlfriend seems to be a positive support, too."

"Ashley is focused and probably leads him down the straight and narrow. I just wonder how long it's going to last."

"Why do you say that?" Sally asked, crinkling her forehead.

"She'll be getting her doctorate next spring. I assume she has some serious career goals."

"I don't believe Brody would hold her back."

"I'm more concerned about her leaving him behind."

"Let's hope that doesn't happen. She seems to be a compassionate person. And working in drug-rehab programs, she knows Brody is in a precarious position. She's been good for him so far."

"I can't disagree with that," John said. "She went with him to Chicago to get his car and other belongings. I guess things are going okay with them."

"This has been nice," Sally said, staring out the passenger window.

John glanced at her. "What's that?"

"Getting away and having some time to talk about things. We don't get to do that enough. I'm excited about this entire weekend. Meeting your friends and spending time with you."

"Did you bring my little blue pills?" he asked with a wink.

"I didn't know that was my responsibility."

"It's not," he said with a naughty grin. "I've got them in my travel bag along with my blood pressure meds."

She squeezed his shoulder. "That's something else to look forward to."

"That's something we can agree on about this trip."

Four

As they pulled into the Paradise Inn motel parking lot, Sally pointed to a marquee sign that read in block letters: "Welcome Back, Riley High School 50th Class Reunion. Class of '68."

"We're finally here," John groaned. "I guess there's no turning back. Unless you want to."

"You're being silly, John. Let's just relax and try to enjoy ourselves. You only have one fiftieth high school class reunion."

"Thank god," John said as eased the SUV into one of the reserved spaces for guest check-ins at the front entrance to the motel. He popped open the rear hatch and looked steely-eyed at Sally. "Ready?"

In unison, they opened their doors and walked around to the back of the vehicle to fetch their luggage. John glanced around the parking lot as several others were unloading their cars. He didn't see any familiar faces.

When they stepped inside, the registration counter was on the right, and a sign-in table for the reunion on the left. John noticed two women sitting behind the reunion desk, each with a red rose pinned to her blouse. They wore fixed cheery smiles. John nodded and went to the registration desk.

After checking in, John picked up the two pieces of luggage as he and Sally walked across the wide foyer to the reunion desk. Pinned nametags with the person's senior-year photo, a class directory, and a sheet showing the times of the various activities planned for the former classmates were on the table. It appeared that about seventy-five percent of the nametags had been claimed.

John pointed at his nametag. "That's me."

"Oh, Johnny," one of the women said, flashing a genuine smile. "You probably don't remember me."

"Uh, let me think," as he eyes gazed toward her nametag with Penelope Byers printed in a clean calligraphy. He forced a grin, unable to put the name with the face, and lied. "It's great to see you, Penelope. It's been a long time."

"You haven't changed that much. I don't recall you with a beard fifty years ago," she said with a nervous giggle. The other woman, with a short, silvery haircut and slender build, sat diffidently, glancing at a yearbook.

John introduced Sally and told the women they needed to go to their room and get refreshed.

"We're having cocktail hour in about forty-five minutes," Penelope said, pointing to the top item on the activity sheet. "It's down by the pool area. We'll see you then."

"I can't wait," John said, trying to sound sincere.

"Oh, Johnny," Penelope said. "I wasn't Penelope in high school. You knew me as Penny. Does that ring a bell?"

"Oh, I recognized you right off the bat. My mind was just a bit hazy from the long drive."

John and Sally proceeded to their room, midway down a long hallway. As they walked past several rooms, they heard chatter and some scattered laughter, apparently old friends getting reacquainted and recalling events dating back a half-century or longer.

The room décor was a throwback to the 1970s with a stained glass swag lamp hanging from the corner, two green accent chairs, a round glass-top coffee table along with two queen-size beds and a small flat-screen TV fastened to the wall over a longer dresser. Except for the TV, everything else had been probably installed when the motel was built and never updated.

"I feel like I'm back to the future," Sally said as she sat on the side of the bed nearest the door.

"You've got that right," John said, as he placed the luggage on top of the dresser. "Really fits the mood of the reunion."

"Do you remember this place?"

"Nope," he said. "And to be honest, driving into town, hardly anything appears familiar. There's more of a sprawl, so maybe we're just not where I used to hang out as a kid."

"Did you remember Penelope at the sign-in?"

"You know I didn't. Even that photo on her nametag didn't ring a bell. Maybe it'll come to me later on."

"How about the other gal?"

"I didn't see her name. But otherwise, I didn't recognize her either."

"I think it said Judith Ratterman, or something like that."

"I really didn't pay any attention to her. The name sounds somewhat familiar. I'll have to give it some thought. I probably should have studied my yearbook before we left home."

"What yearbook?" Sally asked. "I didn't know you had a yearbook."

"It's somewhere in the garage, packed away with my other treasures I plan to donate to the Smithsonian in a few years."

"Well, you should have shared it with me first," Sally said.

"I didn't think about that."

"Why doesn't that surprise me?"

"Because you know me too well."

"We've got almost an hour before the cocktail get-together."

"Why don't we skip it? I'm tired from the long drive and don't feel like socializing."

"Are you sure?"

"Yes, dear. I think I'd like to get out of these clothes and take a shower. Don't forget, I missed my daily nap."

"Maybe you'll change your mind after that."

"I don't think so."

Five

After a shower, John stepped out with the towel wrapped around his waist. Sally was sitting on one of the padded chairs, talking on the phone, oblivious to his presence. He opened his piece of luggage and put on clean underclothes, then sat on the side of the bed and watched Sally's animated conversation, her free hand moving back and forth and head moving up and down, up and down, as if conducting an orchestra.

When it was over, Sally placed the phone on the coffee table. "Whew!"

"Let me guess," John said. "You were talking to Geraldine."

"Mother went on and on about Wendell, Libby, and Brody."

"Brody? What's up with him?"

"She said he asked her for some money and got mad when she asked him what he wanted it for."

"Did she give him the money?"

"Believe it or not, she didn't. Mother said he left in a huff." Sally paused, her mouth tight. "It really upset her."

"Good for her that she didn't give in," John said. "But there's no excuse for him to be rude to her."

"I hope it doesn't mean something bad is going on with him."

"I know what you mean. It's been relatively quiet since he moved in with Ashley. Let's hope it's nothing serious."

"Do you think I should call him?"

"Hell, no." John scowled.

"But what if it's something serious?"

"If it's really bad, he'll get in touch with us. He always does."

"I guess you're right."

"I wonder if your mother told him we were away for the weekend?"

"That didn't come up."

"It's ironic that we were praising him on the way up here, and then he acts like that toward his grandmother," John said.

"I don't think I'll ever understand his behavior."

"So, what about Wendell and Libby?"

"They were wanting to have a small Bible study at the house. Mother didn't want any part of it. I'm sure Wendell wasn't pleased about it."

"Why don't they have it at their place?"

"They told Mother they didn't want to leave her by herself."

"I think Geraldine can take care of herself for an hour or so. She's been alone quite a few times."

Sally shook her head. "I know. It doesn't make sense to me. I wonder if there's something else going on with them?"

"To be honest, I don't like the idea of strangers in our home. I don't care if it's a Bible study, birthday party, pajama party, or whatever occasion. I think they're taking too much liberty while we're away."

"You're right. I don't like it either."

"Would you want me to call Wendell and discuss it with him?"

"I don't believe so. I think Mother will take care of it for us."

"You're right about that. Wendell isn't about to cross his mama."

John pulled back the blanket and sheet and got into bed.

"What do you think you're doing?" Sally asked.

"I told you I was going to take a nap. Would you mind closing that curtain?"

"Honey, it's nearly six o'clock. The cocktail get-together is in thirty minutes. It's too late for a nap."

"Criminy, Sally, let's just stay here and order room service. I know you must be exhausted from the trip. I didn't want to say anything, but you look a little beat. Why don't you shower and join me?"

"I don't think so," she said, hands planted firmly on her hips. "*I'm* going to shower, and then *I'm* going to get dressed, and *I'm* walking down to the pool area so *I* can get acquainted with your classmates. So if *you* plan to join me, get dressed while I shower."

John puffed his cheeks and eased his legs out of bed. "If you say so."

"Yes, I say so," she said, as she undressed at the foot of the bed. "We drove all this way, and I'm not going to let you be a party pooper. Furthermore, this is a gift from Chloe, and I'm not going to let you spoil it. Understand?"

John stood at attention and gave her a hard salute. "Yes, ma'am!"

"Now get dressed," she said, standing in front of him in her bra and panties. "We don't have much time."

"Did I tell you I brought the little blue pills?" he said, flicking his brows.

"Yes, John. Am I supposed to do cartwheels to the shower?"

"Hey, that's mean."

"Now get dressed and behave yourself," she said, disappearing into the bathroom. Seconds later, the shower went on.

John removed pants, polo shirt and socks from his luggage and got dressed. He turned on the TV and tinkered with the channels. Sally stepped out of the bathroom, drying her short white hair with a towel. "You look nice," she said, opening her luggage.

"You look nicer," he said with a wink. "My offer still stands."

Sally ignored him, taking out black leggings and a pink floral top to wear. He turned his attention back to the TV for a few seconds before turning it off.

"John—"

"What?"

"I want us to have a good time this evening," she said. "Don't go with an attitude."

"I won't," he said. "I'll try to be positive."

"That's good to hear."

"But I don't want to spend half the night there," he said. "It's been a long day and we need to save our energy for Saturday and Sunday."

"I've never heard you so concerned about getting tired," she said, giving him a wary eye.

"You're not taking me seriously."

Sally stood in front of the mirror on the wall, tugging at her top and then running a brush through her hair several times. "Okay, that sounds reasonable. We won't spend half the night. I'm sure some of the others are a bit tired as well. We won't overdo it."

"I see there's a golf scramble tomorrow afternoon," he said. "And there's the reunion dinner and dance in the evening."

"What's on Sunday?"

"The activity sheet lists a breakfast on your own in the morning," he said. "In the afternoon, there will be a picnic in the park with several things going on like badminton, croquet, and a softball game. That softball should be interesting in this heat. These old farts will be keeling over if they do that."

"I'm sure the organizers will take that into account on whether or not to play softball."

"It almost sounds like adult daycare," John snickered.

"Now you're being a smart aleck, John."

"Then we can head home on Monday morning. I'm counting the hours."

Sally, acting as if she hadn't heard him, took out a tube of red lipstick from her purse, applied it on her puckered mouth as she stepped closer to the mirror. She smacked her lips several times and smiled.

"How do I look?" she asked, turning to face John.

"Ravishing. I'll be the envy of the reunion."

"Let's not get carried away," she said, picking up her small handbag off the dresser.

"I always get carried away when I'm with you."

"You silver-tongued devil. Let's get going."

"Do we have to?"

"John!"

Six

Midway down the hall as they walked to the cocktail party, John casually reached over and held Sally's hand. She responded with a gentle squeeze. As they turned the corner to enter the pool area, John realized it was the point of no return as a number of classmates turned and watched them enter. He felt his gut tighten, but managed to spread a smile to everyone.

They strode toward the bar, exchanging nods with several people. John didn't recognize a single person, making him wonder for a moment if he were at the right place. If it weren't for the flashy purple-and-gold table decorations signifying the school colors, he may have turned around. If Sally had let him.

It wasn't until he heard someone rushing up behind him, gushing, "Oh, John, is that you?"

John turned as a plump woman nearly fell over in her tracks a few feet from him. "The one and only," he said with a shy grin, trying to read her nametag.

"It's me, Candy," she said with a charming smile. "We were in several classes together. Remember when we dissected a frog in Mr. Ritter's biology class?"

"And you passed out?"

"Yep, and you grabbed me before I could fall and hurt myself."

"It's so good to see you," he said, offering a hand to shake, but instead getting a tight hug from her. A rotund man stood awkwardly behind her with a rigid grin, waiting for the embrace to end. He introduced himself as Willard Kane, her husband, with a spongy handshake. John introduced Sally to them.

"I heard you became a writer," Candy said. "That's so exciting."

"That's stretching it a bit. I was a sportswriter for several years and then became a sports editor in Kentucky. And you?"

"I never left town," she said. "I spent a couple years at a bank and then started having babies. Willard and I have six children and fourteen beautiful grandkids."

Candy opened her purse and pulled out a string of photos of her grand progeny, seemingly having inherited the family's cute and chubby characteristics.

"You've been busy," John said. "We have a son and daughter, and one granddaughter. We haven't been nearly as productive as you and Willard."

John glanced at Sally, and then at his chest, and realized they hadn't worn their nametags.

"I need to run back to the room and get our IDs," he said, as others began trickling into the area.

"You stay here," Sally said. "I'll go back and get them. You socialize."

"Your wife is so pretty," Candy said as Sally walked away. "Have you been married long?"

"We got hitched after college. We're coming up on forty-five years. How about you guys?"

"Right out of high school," Candy said. "So we'll be celebrating our fiftieth in three weeks."

"You sure didn't waste any time."

"We couldn't," Willard said, with a self-satisfied expression and goofy guffaw. "She was beginning to show. You know what I'm sayin'?"

Candy squinted at her husband. "John didn't need to know that."

"Oh, I see," John said, his head slightly bobbing, surprised by what Willard was sharing.

"We couldn't shack up together, because nice folks around here didn't do that back then," Willard said. "Different times."

"You're right."

Candy thumped Willard on the arm. "Willard, would you please stop telling John our life history? You're embarrassing me. I hate to think what John thinks of me now."

"You're not the first to have to get married," John said. "That's just how we did things back then. And you seemed to do fine, considering you're about to have a big anniversary."

"You're so sweet, John. You haven't changed a bit."

"I'm not so sure about that," he said, glancing at the doorway for Sally's return.

"We need to start circulating, Willard," Candy said. "I see a few familiar faces over by the pool. It's so great seeing you, John. Let's talk again tomorrow."

"Sure thing," John said, flashing a grin.

Walking away, John overheard Candy telling Willard, "keep your big mouth shut."

John glanced around the area, moving to the bar. He got a canned beer and walked away several feet while surveying the premises.

"Hey, Johnny," a booming voice came from one of the tables. A tall, overweight, balding man stood and waved for him to come over. "I thought that was you. As goofy looking as ever."

John didn't need to see an ID to know it was Grover Jones, the classmate who had terrorized the school, the infamous class bully most students had tried to avoid. John forced a smile as he approached him.

"Good to see you, Grover," he said. "It's been a long time."

"I'd say fifty years. I don't recall seeing you after we graduated. You high-tailed your ass out of town. We wondered whatever happened to you."

"College, military service, and work. Nothing too exciting. Yourself?"

"Hell, I ended up getting drafted and joining the Marines. I spent a year in 'Nam. Even earned a Purple Heart for getting some shrapnel in my leg. Came back here and never left again. I started a little construction business that's done pretty well over the years."

"Well, good for you," John said, trying to think of something to say to someone he didn't care to talk to. Grover wasn't a person he thought about when he left town, except that he hoped he'd never see him again. It made him think that if he had known Grover was going to be attending, he certainly would have found excuses not to be around him again. If only Sally had allowed him to stay in the room and rest, he thought.

Grover sat on a gray metal chair. "Relax for a minute," he said, picking up a bourbon and water. "Remember the last time we met?"

"That was a long time ago, Grover," John said, tilting his head. "I'm not so sure."

"The hell you don't. Don't try to pull that crap on me. You ain't got that early dementia thing, do you?" Grover let out a huge laugh that drew some attention from those standing nearby.

John gazed around the room, hoping to see Sally and have an excuse to leave. He grinned at several faces, hoping they would come over and interrupt the unwanted encounter with Grover. No such luck.

"You'll have to refresh my memory, Grover. Honestly, I don't recall. A lot has happened since then."

"You don't remember the class party down at the roadside park the night we graduated?"

"So?"

"I squirted beer all over you while you were sitting at a table with some of your loser friends. Does that ring a bell, Johnny boy?"

John let out a light cough. "I think I remember now."

"Bullshit. I know you remember." Grover finished his drink with a gulp.

"So why are you bringing it up? That's more than fifty years ago. A lot has passed since that time."

"I want to let you know I gained a lot of respect for you after that."

John crinkled his eyes. "How so?"

"I admit I used to pick on you a lot," Grover said. "I'm sorry for that. I truly am. I probably shouldn't have called you goofy back then, but you acted kinda goofy at times. But that night, you didn't back down. It surprised the hell out of me when you got up and charged at me with your fists flying in all directions. That was the only time someone fought back at me."

"I don't know what to say," John said with a shrug, taking a small sip of beer. "I was just taking up for myself. That's about it."

"But there's one thing I want to know."

John's brows creased. "What's that?"

"Why did you leave town?"

"Like I told you, I went off to college. I was around town for a couple months after we graduated."

"Did you let all the air out of the tires on my cherry GTO before you left?"

"What?" John arched back. "Are you serious?"

"And did you key my beautiful British racing green automobile?"

"Of course not," John felt sweat trickle down his neck. He took a big swallow of his beer and glanced around the room as if seeking some support from classmates.

"Someone did and a few guys thought it was you because we had that fight. It only made sense. You know what I mean?"

"Well, it sure wasn't me. I'd never do anything like that."

"I wasn't a happy camper."

"I don't blame you," John said. "I'd feel the same way."

"If you say so," Grover said, arching a brow.

John noticed Sally approaching the table, carrying his nametag and wearing hers. He stood, exhaled lightly, and accepted the plastic tag from her.

"Well, hi there, sexy," Grover said as he rose from his seat. "I don't remember you from our class."

"Sally, I'd like you to meet Grover," John said. "One of my classmates from a long time ago."

Sally extended her hand with a pleasant smile. "It's nice to meet you."

"So you're married to this dude?" Grover said with a haughty laugh.

"For nearly forty-five years," she said, flashing John a warm smile.

"Lucky man. Unlucky gal. I think you could have done a lot better, sweetie."

John signaled to Sally with his eyes that he wanted to get away from his old nemesis. "What would you like to drink, honey?"

"I'll have a soft drink," she said.

"It's been nice talking to you," he said to Grover as he took Sally's hand and guided her toward the bar.

"One of your friends?" Sally asked.

"Hardly."

"I sensed that," she said with a small laugh. "Is he drunk?"

"On his way."

"He's a weird character."

"I'll tell you more about him later, if you're interested."

"I'm not so sure."

"It's up to you. It doesn't make any difference to me."

"I'll think about it."

Seven

John and Sally found a vacant table at the far end of the pool to escape from the ever-growing gathering. Several children splashed about in the pool, creating their own shrill loudness that earplugs almost certainly wouldn't mute.

"There's a table with finger foods in the corner over there," John said, motioning with his eyes. "Would you like for me to get us a plate?"

"Let's wait," she said, moving her chair closer to John so they wouldn't have to raise their voices too much to be heard. "Tell me about your friend, Grover."

"So you're interested now?"

"He's part of your past."

"First of all, let me reiterate that he's not my friend," John said, unintentionally raising his voice. "Never has been, never will be. He was the class bully. He just now accused me of deflating the tires and keying his car before I headed off to college."

"Did you?"

"I hope you're trying to be funny. I stayed as far away from him as I could. Lots of kids did back then."

"Does he want to fight you now?"

John laughed. "I certainly hope not. He's still a big buffoon, even though he said he respected me."

"Why?"

"Because I'm a great person," John said with a bogus grin.

"Let's not get carried away."

"The last time I saw him, he poured beer on my head. Although he probably outweighed me by fifty pounds, I'd had enough of his intimidation and fought back. I went after him with all I had."

"That doesn't sound like you."

"Like I said, I was tired of being bullied. I wasn't going to take any more crap from him. I'd like to think I've grown up and don't have to resort to physical fighting to solve problems. In other words, I'm too damn old for that shit."

"So, he didn't bother you after that?"

"That was the last time I saw him until tonight."

"I prefer you as a lover than a fighter," Sally said, gently poking the side of his cheek. "Even though you've always been a bit too laid-back."

"You're telling me after forty-five or so years that I've been a wimp? Thanks a lot."

"You know better than that. I'm just saying there are times when you just let things roll off your shoulders. You know, a little too easy-going."

"Some people would call it grace under pressure."

"You know what I mean."

"I'm sorry I've disappointed you." John looked away, but could feel Sally's sharp stare.

"Mind if we join you?" a man asked. "We need to rest our legs."

"Please do," John said, rising slightly from his chair. They were well-dressed; the man wearing a blue blazer, tan dress slacks, and tie; the woman in a pastel yellow summer dress and white sandals. They seemed out of place, more like attire for an upscale resort party.

"It's been a long time, John," the man said, glimpsing at John's nametag.

"Fifty years." John lowered his head and squinted to read the tablemate's name: Barrett Bozarth. His wife's name was Gloria. He furrowed his brows.

"You might remember me as Barry. We were on the school newspaper together. I was the so-called business manager, although there wasn't much business to manage back then with our mimeographed paper. I seem to recall you were a sportswriter or editor."

"I was just a hack reporter." John chuckled. "Nothing special. What have you been up to since then?"

"I went to college and got a business degree at Penn. I've worked in the banking business since then at various levels. I head an investment group now."

"So you're not retired."

"Too much money to be made to hang it up," Barrett said. "There's easy money out there right now, with a current administration that caters to the big guys, if you know what I mean. They know what drives the economy."

"My guess is you don't live here."

"Heavens no." Barrett took a sip of red wine. "There wasn't a future here. We live in Weston, Connecticut. Didn't you leave as well? I believe I read Lexington, Kentucky."

"That's right. I retired about this time last year. Downsizing at the newspaper, so I accepted an early buyout. I must admit I don't miss it that much."

"I know most of you newspaper folks aren't wallowing in wealth unless on the advertising side and upper management. And from what I've read, there's not much in advertising anymore because of the Internet. The future of newspapers appears to be on shaky ground."

"You've got that right. But I had a good career, so there's no regrets. I'm happy in retirement." He smiled at Sally.

The wives stood awkwardly, weak smiles on their faces, before Sally reached out and shook Gloria's hand.

"My apology," John said, chagrined at himself for failing to introduce Sally. "This is my better half."

"My pleasure." Barrett nodded at Sally with a genial smile and glanced at his spouse. "And this is my Gloria." John shook her wilting hand.

"If you're interested in some investment strategies to pad your retirement in the coming years, give me a call," Barrett said, taking a business card from an inside coat pocket and handing it to John. "It's not too late."

"I'll give it some thought," John said, forcing a smile.

"Gloria and I need to move around and see a few other classmates." They stood and smiled. "It was nice seeing you again. Don't forget to give me a call if you want financial advice."

"Please wait a second," Sally said, taking the small camera from her handbag. "I want to get a picture of you with John."

They stood next to John, all flashing forced smiles, then turned and faded into the crowd.

"I'm not sure if that was a greeting or a sales pitch," John said.

"Did you know him well?"

"Not really," John said with a stiff shrug. "I vaguely recall him at the school paper. I guess Barrett sounds a more business-like than Barry, especially in financial circles. Or maybe not. It does seem a bit pretentious."

"His wife is pretty," Sally said. "Somewhat younger as well."

"Almost young enough to be his daughter," John said. "Must be a trophy wife."

"Don't you think we should circulate a little? People are going to think we're stuck-up or unsociable."

"I guess so."

"John."

"What?"

"I don't think you're a weak person. That's not what I meant earlier. I want you to know that."

"I know." He patted her back. "Sometimes I can be too sensitive. No offense taken."

A soft smile lingered on Sally's face. "Thank you."

"Well, let's go to the food table and mingle along the way, if I recognize anyone."

"And if they recognize you."

As they put veggies and fruit pieces on their plastic plates, John felt a hard nudge in the back. He turned and faced a tall, white-haired man with a long ponytail staring at him with a wily grin. He didn't need to see a nametag to recognize the face.

"You old geezer," John said, with a broad grin as he set his plate on the table. "It's great to see you. Lenny, this is my wife, Sally."

Lenny shook Sally's hand and gave John a hug. "I was hoping you'd show up. You haven't changed a bit except for the beard. It looks good on you. Other than that, a little older, but that's it. Look at me, I've gone to seed."

"No way, Lenny. You've always been thin and had long hair. You were one of the first guys to grow his hair long. I remember Principal Edwards didn't care too much for it."

"You've got that right. He threatened to whack it off with scissors if I didn't cut it. He ended up suspending me for three days because of it. Thank god for the ACLU."

They shifted to the side of the table as other classmates gathered to get finger foods.

"Did you stay here after graduation?" John asked.

"For a few years. I tried my hand at college. That didn't work out, so I played in a band and opened a record store. When that crappy digital music came along, I lost everything. So now I'm just a poor old hippy."

"I'm sorry to hear that. The Internet has been tough on a lot of businesses. I worked at a newspaper that was hard hit. I got lucky and was able to take early retirement."

"So, tell me how's everything else in your life?"

"Two children and a granddaughter. I can't complain. How about you?"

"I lost my missus eight years ago to cancer," Lenny said with a woeful expression. "We never had any kids. It's just me now."

"I know it's something we all have to deal with, even though it's not easy. I've lost a few friends along the way."

"I remember when your mom and dad died in that car accident. That was really a sad day. I really liked them. They treated me so well when I'd drop by your house after school. Made me feel like family."

"They liked you a lot, too," John said. "For the most part, they gave a free pass to my friends. There were a few they tried to keep me from. Mom thought you were funny. I mean, in a good way."

"Those were the days. I sure miss them." A wistful expression enveloped Lenny's lined face. "I wish you hadn't been such a stranger."

"I got caught up in life," John said. "I was in the Army for a couple years, got married, raised the kids, and was involved in my career. Time slips away."

"You've got that right. It seems like only a few years ago we were bumming around town. We were clueless kids just having fun."

"I should have stayed in touch with good friends like you. You think you have all the time in the world until you realize you're running out of it when you get older."

"Listen, buddy, don't blame yourself. It's a two-way street. We all got wrapped up in our own lives and forgot about others. It's a hidden trap we all fall into. But we're still alive and it's great to reconnect, even after fifty years."

Sally maneuvered in front of them and got them to pose for a photo. This time there were genuine smiles.

"I assume you're going to be at the dinner tomorrow night?" John asked.

"Yessiree Bob! I've cleared my busy calendar to make sure I'm there," Lenny said, nudging John with his bony elbow.

"Yeah, me too," John said.

"Hey, man, I need to find the boys' room," Lenny said softly, leaning toward John. "I'm about to pop."

"Understandable."

"It's great meeting you, Sally. I'll see you fantastic folks tomorrow night."

Lenny waved and made a beeline to the exit to locate a restroom.

"Interesting friend you have," Sally said.

"He was one of my buddies. We had some good times back then."

"You'll have to tell me about them."

"Maybe," John said with an impish grin.

Eight

"Honey, are you ready head back to the room?" John asked, seeing Sally cover up a quick yawn. "I hate to admit it, but I'm exhausted. If there weren't all these people here, I think I'd jump into the water and chill."

At that moment, there was a big splash in the pool. They turned around and saw a slender-built man with frizzy gray hair flapping his arms in the water. A crowd gathered next to the edge as the man grabbed the ladder, climbed out, and looked around at the curious onlookers.

"Okay, who's the wise guy?" he demanded. Drenched from head to toe, the man glared at his old classmates. "I don't find it funny."

A man's light chuckle from one of the tables near him. "I'm sorry. I don't mean to laugh. You just look ridiculous standing there. Are you trying to drip dry?"

Several others giggled as the soaked man proceeded toward the table as people parted to let him through. Sitting there was Cecil

Menifee, the student council president his senior year, with another man. Cecil sat with a pleased look as if he were still in a position of popularity.

"How about if I throw your ass in the pool?" the man asked. "Would that be funny?"

"Listen, Virgie," Cecil said in a belittling tone. "Has it occurred to you that you've had too much to drink and you may have fallen into the pool on your own accord?"

"Not when I felt I a hand shove me in the back," Virgie said as stood a couple feet away from Cecil.

"I don't know who would do something like that." Cecil glanced at his friend and shook his head with a slight snort.

"Me either, but someone did. I suppose they're too cowardly to come forward and apologize. I'm going back to my room, change clothes, pack, and leave. I don't know why I came anyway. Some of you were pricks back then, and you're still pricks. And that includes you, Cecil. So you can kiss my ass."

Quiet filled the area for a few seconds before light chatter resumed. Cecil gave his friend a bemused look before taking a swallow from his wine cup.

As Virgie headed toward the exit, John reached out and tapped him on the shoulder. "Don't rush off, Virgie."

Virgie glared at him, an angry squint easing from his eyes as he recognized John. He shook John's hand several times before releasing his hard grip. "Damn, it's good to see you," he said as a large smile creased on his mouth. "Did you see what happened?"

"I saw you in the water, but I didn't see how it happened. Are you okay?"

"Needless to say, I'm royally pissed."

"I don't blame you. Why don't you reconsider, change your clothes, and come back? My wife and I will wait for you," John said, nodding toward Sally. "We can catch up on all the years."

"I dunno," Virgie said, as the throng returned to whatever they were doing before he made his big splash. "Let me think about it." The ink on his nametag had turned to a watery blotch.

"Don't think about it. Just put on some dry clothes and return. We'll wait for you."

"Well, okay then," Virgie said reluctantly with a half-hearted smile before leaving the area.

John got himself another beer while Sally walked over to the side to wait for him. "Tighten Up" by Archie Bell and the Drells played on the speaker system.

"We're going be here a little longer," John said. "Is that okay with you?"

"Of course," Sally said. "I'm not tired like you are."

"Didn't I see you yawn a few minutes ago?"

"That little incident by the pool snapped me out of it."

"Anyway, I don't feel it's right for me to leave after what happened."

"I understand," Sally said, with compassionate eyes. "I feel sorry for your friend."

"Virgie Simpson caught a lot of crap back in school. He got picked on a lot by others. You can see he's not intimidating. He's still scrawny like he was back then. And he didn't have a mean bone in his body. He wouldn't harm a flea."

"How come people bullied him?"

"Let's say he was somewhat effeminate back then," John said. "In other words, they called him a homo or a fag."

"That's awful, John."

"Back in the day, people said those things. It was much worse then than it is now. I remember him being pushed back and forth down the hall between classes. He wouldn't shower after gym class because of guys picking on him."

"Did you defend him?"

John winced, then took a sip of his beer. "I'm ashamed to say I didn't like I should have."

"How come?"

"Immaturity. Gutless. Cowardice."

"That doesn't sound like you."

"Back then, if you came to the defense of a gay person, others would call you gay. Plus, and I know this is an excuse, I felt those things would pass over time. I guess they haven't."

A few minutes later, John noticed Virgie at the door and waved his hand to get his attention. Virgie nodded and walked directly to them as if they were the only people in the room.

"I'm Sally Ross," Sally said, shaking his hand before Virgie could say anything. "I'm John's wife."

"It's a pleasure to meet you, Sally. Johnny was one of my favorite friends in high school, so I know you must be all right," he said with a soft smile. He grinned at John. "You married above your calling, Johnny."

"No doubt about that," John said, flashing a genial smile at Sally. "I'm sorry about what happened at the pool. There was no excuse for it. Let's find a table and talk a bit. Can I get you something to drink?"

"I'm good," Virgie said as they walked to a table opposite where he had fallen into the pool, garnering a few glances from the attendees. "Regardless of what you heard, I only had one glass of wine. And I was pushed. I didn't fall."

"It shouldn't have happened," John said, slowly raising his brows. "But you're okay?"

"Just embarrassed and humiliated, but I'm used to that, being around some of these Neanderthals years ago. Some things never change."

"Unfortunately," Sally said, empathy in her voice.

"I've lost touch with a lot of people," John said. "Did you stay around here?"

"Hell no," Virgie said. "You've got to be kidding. I went to Antioch College and got an art degree, then headed out to Oregon. I've been there since then, except for two or three visits to see family. I can't fathom what made me decide to come to the reunion. I must have a loose screw in my head. Maybe because I've always been curious about what happened to some of our classmates. I can tell you this is my last one."

"This is my first time back here since my parents passed. I've never had much of a desire to come back. Just ask Sally."

"Our daughter paid for this," she said with a light laugh. "Against John's objections."

"But it's not been as bad as I thought it would be," John said. "I've reconnected with a few friends, like you."

"What have you been up to since high school?" Virgil asked. "Anything exciting?"

John repeated what he'd told a few others about his life since high school. "Certainly not as exciting as yours."

"John was a good friend in high school," Virgie said, turning to face Sally. "I don't know if he told you, but high school wasn't a wonderful time for me." Tears welled in his eyes and his mouth tightened for a few seconds.

"I'm a retired schoolteacher, and I can attest to students not having good memories because of mistreatment by others. I even had some unpleasant times when I was in school. I think most of us do. Even the bullies, because they're so insecure. They lash out at others because they don't have the maturity or empathy to deal with others."

"John, and a few others like Lenny, have you met my hippy friend? They didn't judge or anything. And John would include me in different activities. I remember one time they were choosing up sides for a basketball game in gym class, and John picked me. I was a terrible player, but he made sure I wasn't left out. I know it's a little thing, but it was something I never forgot."

"I did that?" John said, surprised by the comment.

"That's what I mean," Virgie said. "You did things without making a big deal. Like it was natural."

"Well, Virgie, I'd like to think it was natural. I never gave things much thought. I just did what I thought was right, and you were my friend. I didn't think it was that big of a deal."

"How people treat others is a big deal. It was back then, and it is now."

"If you don't mind me asking, but did you ever marry or anything?"

Virgie slapped his legs and laughed. "Or anything? To set the record straight, I did get married. In fact, I've been married four times. My first marriage to Lucy ended in divorce. My second wife, Molly, died in a car accident. My third wife, Agnes, ran off with another artist, and we divorced. And my fourth wife, Phoebe, passed away last year from ovarian cancer. So, if you've wondered after all these years, I'm not gay. I was just timid and shy as a teenager."

"I'll admit there was always some talk in school about your sexual orientation," John said. "It didn't matter to me, one way or the other."

"You were too focused on living your own life rather than trying to dictate how others should live theirs. I liked that about you."

"But I should have come to your defense back then."

"That wasn't your responsibility. You were only fifteen or sixteen. We're still developing our minds at that age. Besides, you were a scrawny guy back then as well. You wouldn't have been much help." They both laughed.

"You're right," John said. "It's not easy being a teenager, then or now."

"You might add that it's not easy being an adult, either, in this day and age. There is so much hate and division right now. I remember back when a lot of us thought we could change the world."

"We probably made a few positive changes," Sally said. "Don't you think?"

"Changes for the good and a few negative ones," Virgie said. "I recall back at Antioch when I used to participate in anti-war marches. And then came that awful shooting at Kent State. Lucy and I met at Antioch. We were part of a group that made placards to carry at marches and protests. I remember one time she tore off her top and showed 'Make Love, Not War' in red paint like blood across her breasts. She was a wild woman back then."

"Why did you divorce?"

"Would you believe she became disenchanted with the causes and became enamored with Reagan? She wanted to settle down and have babies. Now she's a right-winger. I've lost touch, but I don't miss her or her politics. Some crazy stuff before and after with her."

"Do you have any children?" Sally asked.

"Since we're adults sitting here, I can tell you I found out I was sterile," Virgie said. "I contracted the mumps when I was in my early twenties. That may have been another reason Lucy was ready to move on to fertile pastures, so to speak."

"Sorry to hear that," John said.

"That's life," Virgie said with a shrug. "I didn't have any children to distract me from my art. I was able to concentrate on painting and sculpting. Furthermore, I'm not sure I would have been a good parent. Too eccentric. It was probably for the best."

"That's a good attitude," Sally said. "Some people aren't cut out to be parents. It's a shame when they find that out after having children."

"You married a wise woman, Johnny."

"She tells me that all the time," John said with a wink.

The crowd began to thin. A few classmates stood by the bar as if expecting last call, while others pecked at the remains on the food trays like hungry birds.

"It appears we're one of the last ones here," Virgie said. "I should probably call it a night."

"Hey, friend," John said. "I'm glad we got a chance to talk. I do hope I'll see you tomorrow."

"I won't sneak out, although I threatened to earlier."

"Promise?"

"You've got my word on it."

"Let me get a photo first," Sally said excitedly, holding up the camera. John moved next to Virgie for the quick snapshot.

Virgie pushed back his chair, gave Sally an unexpected peck on the cheek, gave John a hearty handshake, smiled broadly, and left with a sprightly bounce in his step.

"What time is it?" Sally asked.

John glanced at his watch. "Ten fifteen. Way past our bedtime."

They eased from their chairs and walked to the nearly vacant front foyer. "I wish the restaurant were open," Sally said.

"I'm sure we can find some diner or fast-food place near here if you'd like something to eat."

"If that's okay with you. I know you like your beauty sleep."

"Now you're being a smart aleck, just like your mother," John said with a grin.

They strolled through the lighted, packed parking lot and found their car. A Burger King sign glowed in the distance.

The restaurant was nearly empty except for four teenagers in the corner, laughing and making enough noise for forty people. Sally ordered a hamburger and fries while John got a strawberry shake.

"I've liked your friends so far," Sally said, after they sat as far away from the teens as they could.

"Even Grover?"

"I thought you said Grover wasn't a friend."

"Right."

"Well, I can see he was probably a jerk."

"Probably?"

"But I like Lenny and Virgie."

"They're good guys."

"I took the photo of you and Virgie because I wasn't sure if he'd be back tomorrow."

"If he said he would, he will. Virgie was a man of his word, even back in high school."

"Maybe I can take another one then."

"You're certainly making use of that camera," John said.

"You'll thank me in the future."

"Did you hear Virgie mention that one of his wives died from ovarian cancer?"

"Yes, honey," Sally said. "Let's not go there right now. I prefer to have positive thoughts about Chloe's prognosis."

"I feel the same way."

Sally finished her meal. "I'm suddenly sleepy."

"Me, too. Let's get rested for tomorrow."

Nine

When they returned to the lobby, several classmates were chatting at the check-in table. John didn't recognize any of them as he placed his hand on Sally's lower back to guide her to their room.

"You must be in a hurry to get back," she said.

"I don't want to take any chances of getting lured into some endless talk about long-forgotten times," he said, swiping the card to unlock the room. "I know from experience some old folks go on and on and on about things."

"You as well?"

"I plead the fifth," he said with a laugh. They quickly undressed. John flicked on the TV while Sally went to the bathroom to brush her teeth.

"You feel like TV?" she asked when she returned. "I thought you were tired."

"I'm only channel surfing. I have some nervous energy from the evening. Anyway, I want to get the feel of a remote. It seems like forever since I held one, since your mother moved in."

"Maybe we should get another TV for the bedroom."

"I'm not interested in doing that. Bedrooms are for sleeping and loving. TV takes over when it's around."

"Maybe one in the kitchen or living room?"

"Honey, I don't want another TV. I wish I hadn't said anything about the remote. I don't want my life controlled by a TV. That's kinda like sitting in the rocking chair all day and wasting time doing nothing. I like to be doing things."

Sally snickered. "Okay, I get your point, sir. I wonder how Mother and her company are doing?"

"I would hope they're asleep by now."

Sally pulled back the sheets and they slipped into bed. They rested on their backs, heads propped up by the pillows, and stared at the ceiling.

"This has been a long and interesting day," she said, stretching out her arms several times.

"My friends have taken curious paths in their lives. Some more interesting than others."

"We forgot to do something."

"What's that?"

"Turn off the light."

"I thought you were going to do it," John said, poking her with his elbow. "The switch is by the bathroom door and you were there last."

"You thought wrong, mister. My eyes are too heavy to find the switch. And I'm too tired to get back out of bed."

John laughed. "Women!"

John swung his legs out of bed and went to the door. He heard light chatter and peered through the blurry peep hole and saw Grover and several classmates in the hall. He stood quietly, ear against the door, and eavesdropped on their conversation.

"Did you see Virgie's expression when he fell in the pool?" one of the men asked. "I wish I had a photo of it. That rage on his face."

"I got this on my phone as he was getting out," another man said. "He looks pathetic."

"I didn't mean to push him that hard," Grover said. "I really think he lost his balance."

"Regardless, it was funny. I thought he was going to cry."

"He could have been," a man said. "He was so soaked it would be hard to tell."

"Guys, this is our secret," Grover said in a hushed tone. "Okay?"

"We're cool," a man said, as their voices began to fade as they moved down the hallway.

John turned off the light and tip-toed back to bed, more out of fear of tripping over something in the dark.

"What took you so long?" Sally muttered.

"I overheard a conversation in the hallway. I learned Grover shoved Virgie in the pool."

"Who said that?"

"Believe it or not, but Grover. He said it was an accident. He thought Virgie lost his balance."

"That could have happened, but it's still not right," Sally said as she raised her head slightly from the pillow. "What was the purpose of even touching him?"

"Good point."

"What are you going to do?"

"Hell if I know."

"Are you going to tell Virgie?'

"What good would it do? Don't you think it would spoil the reunion for him and a lot of other people?"

"Maybe so, but wouldn't you want to know if you were Virgie?"

"Sally, you're beginning to sound like an instigator."

"You might be right. I'm not sure if it would do any good to tell him or others."

"Can't we just sleep on it?"

"Okay."

"Let's get through the weekend," John said as he turned his back to her. "I told you I didn't want to come."

"But that wasn't the reason."

"Whatever."

Sally turned and snuggled close to him. "Sweet dreams."

~ * ~

John was awakened by bright sunshine bursting through the patio window as they had forgotten to close the thick heavy curtains. The non-stop whirr of the air-conditioning unit hadn't made for a restful sleep. He turned over, hoping to shield his face from the light, but gave up and crawled out of bed. Sally seemed unfazed, facing the wall, a sheet pulled up to her neck.

John walked to the window, glanced to see if there was any activity, and pulled the drawstrings to close the curtains. He noticed a small coffee maker on the dresser and prepared a cup for himself. The only thing missing from his morning routine was a newspaper to peruse. He remembered to use the app on his smartphone, but after reading the page one headlines, turned it off because it just wasn't the same as holding a physical newspaper. The small print didn't help.

"That smells good," Sally murmured from the bed. "Can you make me a cup?"

"No problem," John said as he rose from the chair.

When the coffee finished brewing, Sally sat cross-legged at the head of the bed.

"Be careful, because it's hot," John said as he handed the small paper cup to her.

"What's on the agenda today?" she asked.

"Nothing much until the dinner and dance tonight. There's the golf scramble in the afternoon. I'm not sure how some of those old farts are going to handle the heat."

"I should have remembered to bring our swimsuits. The pool was so inviting last night."

"Except for Virgie."

"That still upsets me," Sally said, taking a sip of her coffee. "I don't understand why adults would do something like that. Especially old adults."

"Like I said, Grover said it was an accident. Maybe it was."

"So that big bully did it?"

"Apparently so."

"I just better not see him standing near the pool," Sally said, raising her voice. "I'd do more than give him a little push. And I wouldn't be a fraidy-cat about it."

"Honey, he said he didn't mean to do it."

"But that's still no excuse. I'd like to give him a piece of my mind."

"I totally agree, Sally. Let's just let it rest for a while."

"I don't believe you, John."

"What?"

"You sound like you're taking up for him." Sally clamped her mouth.

John stared at her for a couple seconds. "Ready for breakfast? We can go to motel's restaurant."

"I know you're trying to change the subject."

"Very perceptive. You know me well."

"Now you're being a smart aleck." She uncrossed her legs, placed her empty cup on the nightstand, and got out of bed. "And yes, I'm about ready for breakfast. But let me shower first."

"Care for company?"

Sally shook her head incredulously. "I guess. It'll save time."

"And water."

"There you go again."

They peeled off their clothes at the foot of the bed. John adjusted the water temperature before he stepped in and held her hand as she followed.

"Too warm or too cool?" he asked, unwrapping the small bar of soap.

"Just right," she said, turning around. "Back first."

"Anything for my queen."

"How long do you think we're going to be doing this?" she asked.

"Shower together?"

"Yes."

"You don't enjoy it anymore?"

"I didn't say that." She turned around to face him as he lathered the washcloth. "It's just that we're getting older. My body is beginning to sag, especially my boobs. Gravity is really asserting itself."

"Should that matter?"

"I suppose not, but I don't see what's appealing about me."

"It's the intimacy, sweetheart," he said, pecking her on the cheek. "Don't we still share the same bed and occasionally make love? Don't we hold hands? I enjoy the physical closeness we share. One of these days, if we live long enough, we may be content with hugs and cuddles. So, I want to enjoy all of you while I can."

"If you say so."

"Furthermore, I'm not exactly in my prime." He patted his belly. "That doesn't seem to bother you."

"It doesn't make any difference to me. I love you just the same."

"That's how I feel about you, sweetcakes."

"Sweetcakes?"

"I heard that on a TV show the other night," he said with a sheepish expression.

Sally stepped next to him, wrapping her arms tightly around him, placing her head on his chest. "You say the sweetest things."

"Only the facts, sweetheart. Remember, I was a newspaperman."

"For the most part."

"Huh?"

"Virgie?"

"Let me finish that story first. It's still developing."

Ten

John and Sally were seated by a window in the restaurant, providing them a distant view of the Columbus skyline. While not majestic like the ones in New York, Chicago or Atlanta, it was clean and clear, and basically unchanged from his youth in the sixties.

"I remember hanging around the Ohio State campus as a teenager," John said as they waited for their orders. "There were several record shops and used bookstores I'd get lost in for hours. I may have had enough money to buy only one record, but I loved flipping through the album covers and reading the info about the artists. They also had neat posters of protests, arts, and music groups."

"I had a few posters pinned to my walls," Sally said. "Especially the Monkees and Beatles. Remember Bobby Sherman?"

"I think most teens had the Beatles. The Monkees and Bobby Sherman were a little too teeny-bopper to me. I preferred the Stones, Animals, and Yardbirds."

"Mother had my walls painted pink," Sally said. "I even had a Princess telephone."

"Barbie dolls?"

"When I was younger, and I saved my collection. I don't know what happened to them. I suppose Mother gave them away. They would have been valuable now."

"Kinda like my baseball card collection," John said. "I had thousands of cards, but I think my mother tossed them when I went to college or while I was in the military. We could be rich now if it hadn't been for our mothers."

"But they loved us to the moon and back."

"Mind if we join you?" a man asked politely. "I assume you're here for the Riley High reunion." A petite woman with silvery hair and sweet smile stood behind him. "This place is getting crowded."

"No problem," John said, gesturing his hand toward the empty chairs.

The man, tall and slender with a pencil-thin moustache and thick shock of black hair, pulled out a chair for his wife to sit and then sat across from John. He introduced himself as Malcolm Benningfield, and wife Joanne. John saw Joanne smiling at him and tried to avoid eye contact.

"The party at the pool provided some unexpected excitement," Malcolm said. "Do you think someone pushed Virgil in the pool?"

"He says someone did," John said.

"It's a shame something like that happened," Sally said. "It probably spoiled the reunion for him."

"Undoubtedly," Joanne said. "There was simply no excuse for it."

"Malcolm, I'm having trouble placing you," John said. "My memory bank isn't what it used to be."

"Oh, I didn't attend Riley," he said. "I'm here with Joanne."

John studied Joanne's face for a few seconds. "Okay, give me a hint."

"I was a cheerleader," she said. "My maiden name is Bennett."

"It'll come to me," John said. "I really need to see a yearbook to connect names and faces." Joanne scrunched her nose, apparently disappointed he didn't remember her.

"I remember you," she said. "You were quiet and shy. We had a few classes together, but we met before then."

"Did you stay around here after graduation?"

"I went to Otterbein. How about you?"

"I left the state and went to Eastern Kentucky University."

"How come? Ohio State and other excellent colleges are nearby. You just wanted to leave Columbus?"

"It was cheaper to attend a public university in Kentucky than staying here. And yes, I wanted to get away from here and experience other places. It seemed like a big move back then."

"It probably was," she said.

A waitress came to the table, took the Benningfields' orders and refilled their coffee cups.

"How about you, Malcolm? Where are you from?"

"Fort Wayne," he said. "I crossed the border to attend Otterbein. That's where I met Joanne many years ago." He tilted his head and smiled at her. "Best move of my life."

"We've been married almost forty-five years," Sally said. "We're part of a vanishing breed."

"What do you mean?" Joanne asked.

"It seems nowadays a lot of marriages don't last that long. We know quite a few folks who've been married two or three times."

Joanne blushed. "You can probably say that about Malcolm and me. Like he said, we met at Otterbein. We dated some and even got engaged, but he went in the Air Force and I stayed here. I ended up marrying a schoolteacher."

"And I got hitched to a Vietnamese gal while stationed in Saigon and fighting Charlie."

"That's interesting," John said, arching a brow. "I knew a few guys who did that."

"It was more of a humanitarian thing on my part," Malcolm said. "She wanted to flee Vietnam, so I married her and that gave her a ticket to leave. She was a sweet lady, but we had so little in common other than Vietnam. We divorced after five years."

"What happened to her?" Sally asked.

"I really don't know. We went our separate ways. My guess is she's still in California."

"And then you reconnected with Joanne?" John asked.

"Uh, not really," Malcolm said before clearing his throat. "I had some PTSD and drug issues, and went through two more marriages. After extensive counseling in the VA, I finally started getting my life together. For some reason, while visiting my parents in Fort Wayne, on the spur of the moment, I drove over to Westerville to see Otterbein again. I had some time to kill. And that's when I saw Joanne walking across campus. It seemed like a mirage at the time."

"That's so sweet," Sally said, nodding at Joanne.

"It was difficult for a year or so," Joanne said. "I was still married at the time."

"Oh." Sally's head arched back.

"Yeah, we had to sneak around for a while. Then Alvin found out about us. It was rather tense, but we got through it. Right, Malcolm?"

Malcolm chuckled. "You've got that right, hon. I thought he was going to shoot me when he discovered what was going on. But things worked out fine for us."

"If you don't mind me asking, what happened to Alvin?"

"Would you believe that he got remarried about three months after we split?" Joanne said, raising her arms. "Alvin was having an affair with some floozy secretary at the school where he was principal. I couldn't believe it. He got so worked up about me, while he had been unfaithful for who knows how long."

"Interesting story," John said, holding his cup. "I'm glad things worked out for both of you."

"John, I still can't believe you don't remember me," Joanne said. "Have I changed that much?"

"Like I said, I need to see a yearbook to joggle my memory. I'm sure I don't look the same as I did fifty years ago."

"You haven't changed much. Your hair has thinned and you have a beard, but I can look into your eyes and still see you from years ago."

John took a bite of his veggie omelet, chewing slowly, trying to place Joanne somewhere in his schoolboy past. He glanced back at her for a moment, but nothing registered. Meanwhile, the waitress returned with the Benningfields' orders, giving him a little more time.

"Any hints?"

"Do you remember the place we called Teen Town at the community center? It was every Friday and Saturday night, and someone would spin records on a portable player, and all the kids would dance. We were probably freshmen or sophomores."

"I recall going there a few times."

"Well, we were on the teen board together," she said. "Remember?"

"I guess."

"Oh, John, your memory is as bad as Malcolm's." Joanne shook her head. "Anyway, I had the biggest crush on you back then."

"Really?"

"I wanted you to ask me to dance, or out on a date to the movies, or something. But you never did. I used to write about you in my diary or scribble your name on my school notebooks. But you seldom paid any attention to me. You had the reputation of being a good kisser."

"I don't know what to say. I didn't date because I didn't drive a car then. Not much money either."

"Don't you remember that neighborhood theater where kids would go? I think tickets were something like fifty cents," she said. "Boys and girls went there all the time on dates. They'd sit near the back of the auditorium and make out. There was a soda fountain a few doors down where kids would congregate and listen to music on the jukebox."

"I remember those places."

"I think I embarrassed you, John," Joanne said. "I apologize. I was just a lovestruck girl back then."

"I guess I was a clueless teen."

"And after all these years, you still don't remember me."

Sally and Malcom stared at John with bemused expressions, waiting to hear his reply.

John blushed. "Uh, I guess I'm a clueless sixty-something now."

Eleven

As they left the restaurant and entered the wide lobby, John caught a glimpse of Virgie talking to a desk clerk. Virgie must have sensed it as he turned around and John waved.

"Have you guys had breakfast yet?" Virgil asked.

"Just finished," John said.

Virgil's mouth twisted. "Well, darn. I guess I'll have to eat by myself."

"I saw a few other classmates in there. We ate with Joanne and Malcolm Benningfield."

"Doesn't ring a bell."

"She was a cheerleader. Her last name was Bennett."

"I vaguely remember her. She was probably in one of the cliques that didn't have anything to do with the likes of me and others."

"Could be, although she seemed like a nice person," John said. "I still can't place her face and name. It was embarrassing."

"Why don't you go with Virgie and have another cup of coffee while I go back to the room and do a few things," Sally said. "I need to call Mother, too."

"Are you sure?" Virgie asked.

"I'm sure you fellows have some more things to catch up on. Take your time."

"That's especially sweet of you, Sally."

"I'll see you guys later," she said as she walked toward the hallway leading to the rooms.

John headed back to restaurant with Virgie. It was already beginning to thin out. After a waitress seated them, John excused himself to go to the bathroom. He was about to pop from all the coffee and juice he had earlier with Sally. He ordered decaf coffee when he returned, because he'd be a jittery bundle of nerves with more caffeine in his system.

"You know you don't have to be here," Virgie said. "But I do appreciate it. I'm sure you have things to do."

"It's not a problem," John said. "I don't have anything going on now. Sally and I have been killing a little time before going back out later. If not here, I'd be back in the room channel surfing."

"Hey you guys," a man said. "Mind if we join you?"

John and Virgie looked up at Roland Miller and Biff Tipton standing a few feet away with bright smiles. "Sure," John said.

"You get dried off last night, Virgie?" Roland asked as he scooted next to John in the booth. "You got quite a soaking, buddy."

"You were there?" Virgie asked with a long face.

"We were down at the other end of the pool," said Biff, twisting one end of his graying handlebar moustache. "You made quite a splash."

Biff and Roland thought it was a funny quip and chuckled, but John didn't react and Virgie sat stone-faced like a statue.

"It wasn't my intention," Virgie said before taking a sip of his coffee. "I got pushed."

"Really?" Roland asked. "Someone told me you lost your balance."

"Someone told you wrong."

John suspected Virgie, his eyes cast down at the table, was becoming uncomfortable with the comments. "You guys playing golf this afternoon?"

"We brought our clubs," Biff said. "You?"

"I'm not much of a golfer," John said. "Weren't you on the golf team?"

"Good memory," Roland said with a grin. "We finished ninth in the state in sixty-eight."

"I sorta recall that," John said. "Didn't both of you get golf scholarships?"

"You've got that right again," Roland said. "We both went to Ohio University."

"I know you didn't play golf," Biff said to Virgie.

"I had better things to do." Virgie replied softly.

"Swimming team?" Roland said with a laugh.

"Actually, I was on the swimming team," Virgie said with a look of satisfaction. "We won the state in our division."

"I remember that," John said, nodding at Virgie. "That team was something else. I recall some of the members going to Olympic trials that year."

"None of the guys made the Olympics, but it was a great experience for someone sixteen or seventeen," Virgie said.

"Did you guys hang around Columbus after college?" John asked, looking first at Biff and then Roland.

"You know the draft was still breathing down our necks back in seventy-two," Biff said.

"That is another thing I remember," John said. "I'm sure most of us do."

"My father had some connections on the draft board back then."

"And?"

"I never heard from them," Biff said. "But I also enrolled in a seminary school, just to make sure."

"Conscientious objector status?"

"Yep," he said.

"So you're a man of the cloth now?"

"Hell no." Biff laughed. "After the war ended in seventy-five, I traveled around Europe for several years, trying to find myself."

"Did you?" Virgie asked.

"I sure got laid a few times and smoked a lot of hash. That's about all I remember. Kind of a haze now. But when I came back in seventy-eight, I went to law school and I've been lawyering ever since. You might say I'm more of a consultant to the firm now. I try to get my name on as many claims as possible to live comfortably. Did I tell you I have a second home in South Carolina? There's some great golf courses down there."

"You've done all right," John said. "How about you, Roland?"

"I got lucky," he said. "My number was three-hundred fifty or so. I knew they wouldn't get to me. But just in case they did, I was able to get a job at a munitions factory in Indiana. I was considered an 'essential' worker, even though I was a pencil pusher."

"What did you do after that?" Virgie asked.

"You probably don't remember, but my dad owned an investment firm. They gambled on me and I worked there for a number of years. Now, like Biff, I'm retired. My wife and I live near Hamilton so we can be close to our grandchildren."

"Weren't you Rollie back in high school?" John asked.

"I haven't been called that in years," Roland replied curtly.

"Weren't you a sportswriter, John?" Biff asked. "That must have been a great life."

"After the military and college, I became a sportswriter. I retired a year ago as sports editor of the newspaper in Lexington. I don't have many regrets."

"Damn, but it must have been something going to all those sporting events and having a front-row seat."

"My seat wasn't always front row," John said with a laugh. "Those were reserved for the reporters for the *New York Times, Washington Post*, Associated Press, *Chicago Tribune* and *Los Angeles Times*. But it's not as glamourous as it appears on the surface. You're out there hours before the start of a game, and then you have to file stories long after it's over."

"I never thought about that," Biff said.

"And you were in the military?" Roland asked.

"I spent a couple years in the Army, including a year in 'Nam. Something I'll never forget but wouldn't wish on anyone."

"Oh."

"I know you didn't serve," Biff said, turning his gaze at Virgie.

Virgie tilted his head. "Why do you say that?"

"Uh, you know."

"I don't know what you're talking about," Virgie said, his face turning red.

"What happened"

"I was like Roland. My draft number was high. And I was married."

"Married?"

"I didn't stutter."

"I didn't know that."

"Now you know."

"Uh, Biff, we better get our stuff together and head out to the golf course," Roland said as he eased off his seat. "We don't want to miss our tee time."

Biff glanced at his watch. "No shit, Sherlock. They'll be teeing off soon."

"I hope you guys have decent rounds," John said.

"We'll tell you about it later," Roland said before he and Biff dropped several bills on the table for their food and scurried away.

"I'm sure they will," John said, after they were out of earshot. "There's nothing more boring than someone recalling every single drive and putt. Like it really matters."

Virgie laughed. "You don't have to worry about me ever doing that. I don't recall the last time I picked up a golf club."

"You were occupied picking up artist brushes," John said.

"Roland didn't finish telling his life story," Virgie said. "He left out some important details."

"What's that?"

"He got caught in some kind of Ponzi scheme and served five years in prison. I was surprised he showed up at the reunion, since a lot of folks remember what happened. It was big news on TV and newspapers."

"I kinda recall when it happened, but Roland's name didn't register at the time."

"He was the alleged ringleader," Virgie said. "Another reason he moved to Hamilton was because his name was mud around here."

"I'm surprised Biff is hanging around him."

"Besides being on the golf team, Biff also represented him in court. That may be a reason Biff has a place in South Carolina."

"You're probably right about that."

"Ready to go? I'm sure Sally is wondering what's been up with you."

"Probably so," John said. They paid at the register and left as the restaurant staff was transitioning to the lunch crowd as several workers were setting up the buffet line.

"I'll see you at the dinner," Virgie said as he departed for his room. "And thanks for the lively conversation."

Sally was sitting next to the patio window when John returned to the room. The housekeeping staff had already made the bed and tidied up the room.

"You must have had lots to talk about," she said.

"We had couple guys drop by and talked about various and sundry things. It was interesting."

"I called Mother, and she's doing okay. She said Wendell and Libby were doing a Bible study at their house and would be back soon. She also said Brody dropped by again and even spent some time with Whiskers."

"So all's fine on the home front. That's reassuring."

"Brody even brought Ashley with him, so things must be going well."

"I hope that's what it means. You never know with Brody."

"Mother did say that she talked to the 'colored girl' while Brody was out with Whiskers."

"Oh, geez. I can't believe what comes out of her mouth sometimes."

"She also thought Ashley had a healthier appearance."

"Maybe it'll carry over to Brody. He could use a few pounds."

"As a matter of fact, Mother said Ashley appeared a little heavier and had a nice glow about her."

"The face of a drug-free life."

"Let's hope the same for Brody. I'm crossing my fingers."

"Brody didn't ask her for money again?"

"Mother didn't mention it. That's not to say she didn't give him some."

"Once an enabler, always an enabler."

"That's not nice, John. She is his grandmother, and she's entitled to do some things for her grandchildren."

"Regardless of age?"

"Regardless of age."

"I can see I'm not going to win this argument."

"I also talked to Chloe and everything is fine there. Whitney is adjusting well to the first grade."

"Did she say anything about visiting?"

"Maybe next month when Whitney is on fall break. She has to work things out with Samantha."

"What do you mean?"

"They've split up again," Sally said with a crooked mouth. "Maybe for good this time."

"Boy problems?"

"I think so. She told me she'd tell me more when we get back home. She didn't want her problems to distract from the reunion."

"That's Chloe," John said. "Always putting the family first."

"Sometimes I wish they would go their own separate ways. I think a lot of Sam, but she seems to keep everything in a minor uproar. It's not fair to Chloe or Whitney."

"I see where you're coming from," John said. "But they're adults. They'll work it out."

"You think?"

"I'm trying to be positive, Sally."

"I know," she said with a tiny smile. "So what are our plans for the afternoon?"

"I thought we might drive around to the old high school and check out the neighborhood."

"Maybe I can learn some more things about your hidden past."

"There's not much to find out about me."

"I found out this morning that you were a terrific kisser."

"But you already knew that," he said with a devilish grin before blowing her an exaggerated kiss.

Sally rose from the chair. "I think we better get going before you get something else on your mind."

"You're reading my mind."

"That's not too difficult."

"Oh, being a smart aleck again."

"Just dishing it back out to you. Let's go!"

"Yes ma'am, after I go to the bathroom."

Twelve

The traffic was light as they drove toward downtown Columbus, but it would be picking up over the course of the afternoon to bumper-to-bumper as fans flocked to Ohio State. The Buckeyes had a football game against the Purdue Boilermakers at Ohio Stadium that evening.

"Did you ever regret not going to school here?" Sally asked.

"I guess to some extent, because it was close to home and several of my classmates decided to attend," John said. "But, like I've told you and others, I wanted to get away from home and see something different. I got a good education at Eastern Kentucky that served me well. I always believed that college was only as good as what you put into it. Some of the best journalists I knew came out of public colleges. And, furthermore, I wouldn't have met you if I had gone to OSU."

"You don't believe destiny would have pulled us together?"

"Are you being serious?"

"Not really," she said. "But I know some women who believe there is only one man they are predestined to love."

"I've heard guys say it as well about the women they fell for."

"Lovestruck."

"That sounds more like a romance novel to me," John said as they waited at a stoplight.

"You're right. But it's a sweet fantasy, especially for someone who has been with one person all their life."

"I can see where they would believe that then."

"It still appeals to the romantic side of me," Sally said. "I guess I'm old-fashioned. I still like to believe we were made for each other."

"I'd like to think there's something to that because we've been together for so long," John said. "But I think it's more the case of us making it work, through the ups and downs. And let me add, we've had a lot more ups than downs."

"And a few thicks and thins, too."

"And whatever else."

"Always the realist," she said. "But I see your point. I just like to think there's some magic involved as well."

"Maybe that magic is simply lust."

"Oh, John, only you would say something like that."

"Seriously, don't you think a lot of folks simply fall in lust at first sight?"

"Then I'd say it's not love, only physical attraction that won't last a lifetime."

"I don't disagree. That's a reason the divorce rate hovers around fifty percent."

"I don't think it was only lust between us at the beginning, unless I misread you."

"I'll only say that I found you physically attractive when I first met you," John said. "But the deciding factor was your personality. I enjoyed being with you."

"I see what you mean," she said. "I found you physically attractive as well."

As they crossed the Main Street Bridge, over the Scioto River, the Columbus skyline stood out against the bright blue sky. The LeVeque

Tower and its art deco design stood out impressively from the other buildings.

"This bridge is new," John said. "When I lived here, there was an art deco-style bridge spanning the river."

"This is really a beautiful city," Sally said.

"A lot of people don't realize how large it is," John said. "They generally believe Cleveland and Cincinnati are the largest cities, but Columbus is the most populous. Cincinnati may have a slightly larger metro area, if you include northern Kentucky. I think Columbus is second only to Chicago in the Midwest."

"I didn't know that either."

"But Cincinnati and Cleveland have something Columbus doesn't."

"What's that?"

"Major League Baseball and National Football League teams. That bothers some of the locals."

"That's understandable, I suppose."

"But the city does have National Hockey League and Major League Soccer teams. Some would argue that Ohio State is professional, too, like so many other universities."

"Interesting," Sally said, followed by a yawn that John noticed. Although he had spent most of his life in sports, she wasn't particularly a sports fan, although she would accompany him to a game once in a while if she'd liked the city. Generally, she would go shopping, visit a museum, see a movie, or wait in the hotel room with a good book while he worked.

"We should really come back here when we have a lot of time to explore. It has a world-class zoo, some wonderful museums, a great botanical garden, and, of course, an outstanding university. Did you know zookeeper Jack Hanna is the director emeritus of the zoo?"

"I didn't know that," she said.

"I'm a fount of insignificant information."

"I know," she said with a chuckle. "I've learned so little from you."

"Being a smart aleck again?"

"You love it!"

"There's a lot to explore here."

"We'll put it on our bucket list for a long weekend getaway."

They drove quietly on East Broad Street for ten minutes, listening to the radio, glancing at the old buildings and neighborhoods that bore the influence of German and Italian heritage. John pulled to the curb by a small park that had two basketball courts, three small picnic shelters, and a Little League baseball field. Four boys were playing basketball on the netless goals.

"This is it." John said.

"What?"

John pointed to a rusty metallic sign at the entrance to the park, leading to a parking lot by the baseball field. "Riley Memorial Park."

"My high school is now a park," John said. "I thought there would be more than a sign here, perhaps a building or gymnasium. It's all gone."

"I'm sorry."

"No biggie," he said. "Time marches on. The school was old when I attended. Out with the old, in with the new. At least it's a playground for the neighborhood to use. All is not lost."

"But I don't see anything new."

"I'm sure there's a nice high school somewhere around here."

John drove several blocks from the park and stopped across the street from a two-story frame house with a narrow driveway. A tall oak tree provided shade for the green wood-plank porch that had a swing.

"I remember this place," Sally said with a smile. "It hasn't changed much since you brought me here to meet your parents."

"The owners have taken good care of it," John said, as a smile eased across his face. "There's a lot of memories here."

John got out of the car, held up his smartphone and snapped several photos. He stared at the house for several seconds, lost in thought about his childhood days.

A middle-aged man, bare-chested, wearing checkered Bermuda shorts and holding a can of beer, stepped out on the porch. "May I ask what you're doing?" he yelled. "This is a private home, ya know."

John held up his hand and smiled. "I don't mean to intrude. That's my childhood home."

"Oh," the man said. "Okay then. Take all you need." He stepped back inside the house, but John could see his silhouette through the screen door.

John thought for a moment about asking if he could go inside, but decided against it since the man didn't offer or seem welcoming. He walked across the street and clicked several more photos at different angles. John waved at the man, assuming he was still by the doorway, and returned to the car.

Back in the SUV, he glanced at the house one more time, and slowly drove away. He knew it would probably be the last time he would see the old homeplace. Sally didn't say a word, allowing him to savor his memories from long ago.

Thirteen

"Getting hungry?" John asked as they got on East Broad Street and headed toward downtown.

"A little," Sally said. "We still have a lot of time before the dinner and dance."

"I wonder who came up with that idea? I can't imagine too many people wanting to dance. They'd rather sit around and reminisce about the supposedly good old days."

"Always the curmudgeon."

"You've got that right."

"You know I'm right."

"You weren't involved in the organizing, so how do you know?"

"Gimme a break, Sally," John said. "Most of us don't move around like we did fifty years ago. I wonder how many have arthritis? Maybe some have had hip- or knee-replacement surgeries. I bet a few have had heart attacks. There's probably other ailments that prevent them from dancing. And maybe folks don't want to dance."

"Please, John, I think you're exaggerating to make a point. Sure, some people may not get out there and do the Twist or whatever, but they might like to slow dance, regardless of their physical condition. Right?"

John shook his head. "I give up."

"So where do we eat?"

"Let's go over to Germantown Village. There are a few quaint restaurants there as well as some neat shops we can browse. At least there used to be."

"Back in the good-old days?"

"You're getting more and more like your mother as you grow older," he said, shaking his head in mock disgust.

"Now those are fighting words, mister!" She balled her hands into fists at him.

The traffic grew more congested as they approached Germantown Village. They noticed quite a few pedestrians walking around in scarlet-and-gray outfits, dressed in Ohio State colors for the upcoming football game.

"I think we'd better find another place to stop," John said, who, as he had grown older, always tried to avoid large crowds and heavy traffic.

"You're the pilot. I'm the passenger."

As the incoming traffic toward Ohio Stadium grew heavier, John whisked in the opposite direction to where the motel was located. Several cars had fan flags attached to the windows, a vast majority supporting the Buckeyes. He pulled off at an Italian restaurant that didn't appear inundated with customers.

John requested a carafe of red wine after they were seated at the corner table. Sally placed an order for baked spaghetti, while John got eggplant parmigiana. The waiter also brought a basket of six breadsticks, something John tried to avoid and Sally usually devoured.

"I wonder how the golf outing is going?" John asked. "It's not quite as hot as it was coming up here yesterday."

"We'll find out a little later. They may end up in the motel pool before the dinner."

"You know, this was probably a bad weekend to hold a reunion, with the football game and all."

"Columbus seems large enough to handle football fans and the Riley High School reunion."

"Yep," John said. "I suppose Ohio State couldn't reschedule the game to avoid the conflict."

"That would have been the proper thing to do."

"You're getting about as sarcastic as me."

"I can't imagine why."

"Ain't it fun?" he said, fluttering his brows like Groucho Marx.

"Did you have any African Americans in your class?" Sally asked.

"Sure. Why?"

"I didn't see any last night or around the motel this morning."

"We didn't have a lot. Back then, a lot of folks moved outside of Columbus to escape desegrated schools. It wasn't until the late seventies that busing was ordered by the courts."

"Sounds a lot like Kentucky."

"Probably in most places around the U.S. That seems like ages ago. I'd almost forgotten about it."

"Now we have all the private schools to separate students," Sally said.

"Racially and financially."

"And religious separation."

"It seems like these private schools only take minorities who are rich, academically outstanding, or terrific athletes," John said.

"And along the way, government has reduced funding for public schools."

"As some have said, the dumbing-down of America."

"Sad. I'm glad I retired when I did," Sally said.

"We sure have interesting conversations," John said. "How did we get on this subject?"

"I mentioned African Americans."

"I don't think I ever told you, but several weeks ago, I was chatting with Wendell about politics and he said it didn't really matter to him who was elected because it really didn't affect him."

"You should have known better," Sally said as she picked up a breadstick. "He's not going to rock the boat."

"I explained to him that things may not affect him in the short term, but rhey could have enormous impacts on his children, grandchildren and future generations. Issues like air quality and clean water, or preserving national parks and federal lands."

"What did he have to say?"

"He'd never thought of it that way."

"That's Wendell."

"But rather than argue, he thought God would take care of everything."

Sally sighed. "My poor brother."

"Maybe there's still hope for him."

"I'm not so sure."

"I guess he believes more in the power of prayer than in the power of the ballot box."

"Amen."

Their food arrived, and they enjoyed their meals while light Italian instrumental music played softly in the background. The serenity was broken when a boisterous group of football fans decked out in Purdue's gold-and-black colors entered the restaurant.

"I think it's time to go," Sally said.

"How about if we go to the motel and get a nap in?"

"That works for me."

John paid for the meals and they headed back to the motel. The lobby was busy as people were checking in at the front desk and bellhops were scurrying back and forth with luggage carts. Most of the check-ins appeared to be in town for the game.

As they worked their way through the crowded throng, John felt a tightened grip on his forearm. He turned and faced Tyrone Brune, one of his Black classmates. Tyrone was tall and thin, not having changed much since his playing days as star basketball player for the Riley Rebels. He was bald except for thin graying strips of hair on both sides of his head, but still appeared fit for a pickup game.

"You sonofagun," Tyrone said, giving John a bear hug. "I was hoping you'd be here."

"I was wondering where you were," John said. "I didn't see you at the little gathering last night."

"Hey, man, we drove here from Chicago. There were traffic delays all the way through Indiana. We ended up spending the night in Dayton."

John introduced Sally, and Tyrone did the same with his wife, Maggie. "Let's go to the lounge and get a cold drink," John said.

"Do you think there might be room in the restaurant?" Tyrone said. "I could use a big, tall glass of sweet tea and a little something to eat."

"Let's go see."

They were able to get seated at a booth. Tyrone and Maggie opted for the salad bar with their iced teas, while John and Sally, still satiated from their Italian dinner, ordered coffee and split a slice of pecan pie.

"So what in the world have you been up to all these years?" John asked after they returned from the salad bar. "You look great."

"Mind if we pray?" Tyrone asked solemnly, taking hold of Maggie's hand and bowing their heads. John and Sally did likewise during the silent meditation.

About fifteen seconds later, Tyrone raised his head and smiled. "You know I went to Iowa and played basketball, then I bounced around in the Continental League for a few years. I never could make the jump to the NBA."

"That's always easier said than done."

"Anyway, I met Maggie in Rapid City and decided it was time to give up on my dream of playing in the NBA. But I found a bigger dream when I did that."

"Really?" John asked with crinkled brows. "What was that?"

"I got involved in God's ministry. We relocated to Chicago and I work with inner-city residents, spreading the love of Christ and helping them resist all the devil's temptations. Let me tell you, John, it's a wicked world out there."

"Oh," John paused. "Uh, it sure is."

"Hey, brother, I know what you're thinking, but we do more than preach the gospel. There's lot of problems in the cities like gun violence, drugs, and health issues. Having that faith in God is one thing that brings a lot of people together. It's where they can find some peace in their lives."

"Amen," Maggie said, taking a stab at her salad.

"That's certainly interesting," John said. "And challenging. You must get a lot of fulfillment from that."

"It fills our souls," Tyrone said with a warm smile, "every time we save a soul."

"Hallelujah," Maggie said. "Praise the Lord."

"My brother works in a ministry back in Lexington," Sally said. "It's not quite the level of what you do."

"It's more walking around neighborhoods and handing out pamphlets and conducting Bible studies," John said. "Minor league compared to what you do."

"Listen, John, it's all important, big or small. We all do what we can do for the Lord. Your brother-in-law is a valiant warrior in God's army."

"Amen," Maggie said, glancing upward. "Praise the Lord."

John closed his eyes as if in a dreamy trance as the tune "Onward Christian Soldiers" suddenly resonated in his head.

"What have you been up to since high school?" Tyrone asked, snapping John out of his momentary escape. "It's hard to believe it's been fifty years. Where has the time gone, brother?"

John briefly recounted his time in the military, college, career in newspapers, and family, something that was well rehearsed from talking to other classmates. He noted that Brody had lived for several years in Chicago, but didn't divulge his son's drug problems.

"You've sure had a productive life, John. You've been blessed in many ways."

"I can't deny that," John said with a small smile. "We're thankful every day. Right, Sally?"

Sally blinked her eyes and nodded, as if she'd been daydreaming, too. "We've been blessed."

"I always appreciated that you and some of our classmates accepted me back at school," Tyrone said. "There was still some hatred back then against Black folks. That was during the Civil Rights days and Dr. Martin Luther King Jr."

"I don't know what to say."

"Your parents did a good job raising you."

"Well, they were open-minded and never had a racist bone in their bodies."

"You probably don't know this, but going home with you back in middle school was the first time for me in a white man's home."

"I remember we'd play basketball back in the alley behind the house. Dad put up a goal post, backboard, and rim. Those were good times."

"Your mom would invite all of us for Kool-Aid and cookies in the kitchen. Sometimes we'd go up to your bedroom and read your Superman comic books."

"I remember," John said, with a faint smile as he thought back to those childhood days.

"Is there something on your mind?" Tyrone asked.

John smiled. "I was just thinking about the time I stayed overnight at your house. That was the first time I'd ever spent in an African American home. I didn't give it any thought at the time. We were just friends."

"Whatever happened to your parents?"

"They were killed in a car accident several years back. They were only in their early sixties. I still miss them after all these years."

"I'm sure you do," Tyrone said with a warm expression. "My father died in the Korean War. I hardly knew him. My sweet mama raised three of us kids."

"I didn't know that about your dad. That must have been difficult for you growing up, especially back in the fifties and sixties."

"My mama was a strong woman. She made sure me, Charles, and Bernice walked the straight and narrow. Made us go to church, too, every Sunday, Wednesday, and revival meeting. Lordy, it seemed like church was my second home. She wouldn't take any nonsense from us because she knew how things were back then for Black folk. She passed a few years ago. Oh man, was she an angel on Earth."

"Amen," Maggie said, taking a napkin and wiping a tear from her eye. "She was like a mother to me, too. I loved that sweet woman."

"How about you, Sally?" Tyrone asked. "Did you have good parents?"

"My dad died a few years ago," she said. "My mother is still alive. In fact, she lives with us in Lexington."

"You are truly blessed."

"I know." Sally's eyes welled. "Sometimes I take her for granted."

"She won't be around forever, you know," Tyrone said. "Unless in your heart."

"Do you still have your parents, Maggie?" Sally asked.

"Daddy was a policeman and he was killed on duty," Maggie said. "Momma got down with the flu a few years back and didn't make it."

"I'm so sorry," Sally said.

"Tyrone, I bet you could still go out and play basketball," John said.

"Not with these knees," he said with a laugh. "The doctor said I need to have knee-replacement surgery on both knees, but I'm holding out."

"Medicare should cover it."

"I just don't want to be confined to my apartment when there is so much of the Lord's work to be done."

"Doesn't the Lord take care of those who take care of themselves?"

"Clever, John," Tyrone said with a laugh. "But the Lord will let me know when it's time for me to have that operation. Is your health okay?"

"Some ticker scares, but otherwise, I'm fit."

"Prostate too?"

"So far."

"I've had prostate cancer. The doc caught it early, so I'm in good shape. We old guys have to watch out for that."

"I have it checked every year. My PSA has been good."

"Don't let that fool you, John. I thought mine was good until the doctor did his physical exam. It ain't fun to bend over, but it's the best way."

"I'll keep that in mind."

"You know, John, I find myself preaching all the time, even though I don't mean to. Here I am telling you about cancer and how to live, and I know you can handle it yourself. We've been through a lot and learned a lot over the years."

"I guess it's just a hazard of the profession," John said. "Once a preacher, always a preacher. But you're forgiven." He winked.

Tyrone let out a hearty laugh that caused several people at nearby tables to turn and look in their direction.

"I'm looking forward to tonight and seeing old friends," Tyrone said. "I hate to leave good company, but I need to take my afternoon nap."

"I do the same thing, so don't apologize," John said.

"Can we pray before we depart these premises?"

"Go ahead."

"Let's hold hands," Tyrone said, reaching over and clasping John's and Maggie's hands while Maggie clutched John's and Sally's hands. "Dear Lord, thank you for your blessing of friendship that carries us through life's joys and sadness. We pray that you will look out for us as we are about to reunite with old friends later today. We pray this in your holy name."

"Amen," Maggie said, lifting her head with a smile.

"Amen," John and Sally said softly in unison.

"Praise the Lord," Tyrone and Maggie said, both gazing up toward their heaven.

Fourteen

"Tyrone is a fascinating guy," John said as he and Sally sauntered down the hallway to their room. "I would have never guessed him to end up being a minister when we were in high school. He was always quiet and somewhat shy, except on the basketball court where he was an exceptional player."

"Do we ever really know someone when they're only sixteen or seventeen?" Sally asked as John unlocked the door. "We're still developing as people."

"I'm sure you've been more cognizant of that as a teacher. But I understand what you're saying. I didn't have a clue about my life, really, until I finished the military. I was more focused then."

"But didn't you major in journalism in college?"

"Yeah, but I really didn't understand what it was all about, other than what I read in newspapers. I liked to write so it seemed like a good fit. Did you think you'd end up as a teacher?"

"To be honest, yes," she said, as she stripped to her bra and panties. "I belonged to the Future Teachers of America, so that gave me somewhat of an idea about it. And back then, there didn't seem to be as many career choices for women. We became teachers, nurses, or secretaries. That changed a lot in the seventies with the feminist movement. But getting back to your question, I admired and loved my teachers and wanted to be one. They were big influences on my life."

"Uh, why did you take off your clothes?"

"I thought we were going to take a nap before the reunion dinner. I didn't necessarily want to get in bed with my clothes on. Did you have something else on your mind?" She pulled back the sheets and got in bed as the air-conditioner worked overdrive pouring out frosty air.

John chuckled. "I didn't until you started taking off your clothes. Mind if I join you?"

"Only if you have sleeping on your mind."

"Now that's not fair," John said as he removed his pants and shirt. "How can you expect me to be that way when lying next to a sexy woman like you?"

"Keep that up and I may change my mind," she said as he tumbled in next to her. "A girl can handle only so much flattery."

"Are you saying you'd like to hear some more?" He wrapped an arm around her waist and pecked her on the cheek.

"You'll know when I've heard enough."

Sally turned on her side, facing him, and they exchanged soft kisses in their gentle caress.

"Would you mind if we rested for a few minutes?" John asked.

"Did you forget your little blue pills?"

"No. And for the record, I don't need them all the time. You know that. You're my major turn-on."

"So why do you want to rest?"

"Well, er, this bed is so comfortable right now. Being out today in the hot sun and driving around the city kinda wore me out. I feel drained, for some reason. And the pecan pie in my belly doesn't help."

"You were the one who wanted to make love."

"I do, but after I rest up," he said. "I want to be at my best for you." He couldn't suppress a laugh after that comment.

"John, I don't believe you," she said, jabbing him in the belly with her forefinger, causing him to lurch back. "You can be so full of it at times."

"A guy has to have a good excuse for putting off an opportunity like this."

"If you say so." Sally turned over, placing John's hand on her smooth belly. "I'm tired as well. But do one thing."

"What's that?"

"Can you change the setting on the air-conditioner? I'm freezing." Sally pulled the duvet up to her neck.

"That I can do." John slipped out of bed, changed the setting on the air-conditioner, and scrambled back to bed, snuggling next to Sally.

Within minutes they were both asleep, only to be disturbed by a gentle knock on the door. John climbed out of bed and put on his pants, only to be greeted by a housekeeper handing him several clean towels she had neglected to leave when she had made the room while they were away. He put them on the bathroom counter, stripped, and slipped back into bed.

Ten minutes later, the phone rang. He picked it up on the third ring and heard a recorded announcement about the restaurant's dinner specials that evening.

After another ten minutes, he heard cars blaring their horns in the parking lot. He opened the curtain several inches and saw a small caravan of cars, all with Ohio State fan flags, apparently on their way to the game. He glanced at Sally, who was napping soundly and oblivious to all the booming noise.

Whatever intentions John had simply vanished in thin air. He had passed his threshold for falling asleep and wasn't about to disturb Sally's slumber for any physical pleasure. At least right now. He put on his pants and shirt and stepped out to the hallway with no purpose other than to explore the motel property by himself.

That lasted only as far as the gift shop in the lobby, where he ran into Virgie at the magazine stand.

"Exciting day?" John asked.

"I stayed in the room most of the time, watching TV and reading. Even managed a short nap," Virgie said. "How about you?"

"Sally and I drove over to the old neighborhood. Did you know the high school had been razed?"

"I heard that happened a few years ago. My mom told me about it."

"There's a park there now."

"I may go over there tomorrow and check it out."

"Have you seen anyone else from our class?"

"Remember Judy Ratterman?"

"Other than seeing her at the registration table last night. I really don't recall her."

"About the same with me. I was over here earlier to pick up something for lunch and stood next to her in line. It was weird."

"How so?"

"I was trying to be friendly and made a comment that we had a few classes together. She hardly acknowledged me other than saying, 'I know.' That was it."

"Nothing else?"

"It was almost like I wasn't there. She paid for whatever she was buying and left without saying another word." Virgie sniggered. "It made me wonder if I needed a deodorant or something. It felt awkward."

"If it makes you feel any better, she didn't speak to me either last night. Do you know anything about her?" John asked as they stepped outside the shop.

Virgie tilted his head in thought. "You know, when I think about it, I don't think she finished the school year with us."

"Her family moved?"

"That's probably it. I could be wrong, but it seems like she didn't return after Christmas break."

"Was she popular?"

"I'm not sure. She was part of that clique of students who thought they were smarter than others."

"I was probably more of an outsider. I didn't run around with that many students. And I certainly wasn't part of that smart clique. I barely got through by the skin of my teeth."

"Same here," Virgie said. "I spent time at school with art students. People kept away from us because they thought we were strange. Or queer."

John let out a laugh. "I never heard that, but it wouldn't surprise me."

"Believe me, it happened."

They walked outside the front entrance and sat on a bench to the side under an aluminum cover, near a concierge station that appeared to be long abandoned.

"Remember when we were freshmen and thought we would start a band?" John said. "I think it was you, me, Alex, and Stan."

"That was after the Beatles and Stones, and every guy wanted to be in a band if they weren't good in sports."

"And to impress the girls."

"They seemed to like the boys in the band."

"Stan had a set of basic drums and we had guitars," John said. "My dad let me have his that had been in the basement. I couldn't play a lick."

"I think I got one from a second-hand store. It was out of tune all the time...even after trying to tune it, it never sounded right. Alex thought he could just strum the strings and sing."

"Alex could hardly carry a tune either, but at least he tried."

"We were awful."

"And we tried to sound British."

"I'm sure those Midwestern English accents fooled a lot of people," Virgie said with a chuckle.

"What's funny is that we saw the Beatles on Ed Sullivan and thought it would be easy to play instruments. It was later that I found out the Beatles had been playing together for seven or eight years before hitting the big time."

"We thought we could take a short cut. Did you ever learn to play the guitar?"

"Hell no," John said. "My parents even arranged for some lessons that lasted a few months. I never got the hang of it. I guess if I had practiced more, it might have helped. How about you?"

"Same here."

"I wonder what happened to Alex and Stan?"

"Alex joined the Marines after high school," Virgie said. "He never came back. Last I heard he was missing in action."

"That's so sad. So young. He must have been only eighteen or nineteen."

"Alex and I had several classes together. He was always gung-ho about going to 'Nam."

"And he didn't return," John said, shaking his head. "That's so depressing, when you think about all he missed in life. He was still a kid. Life can be so unfair."

"Stan did stay in music for a few years. He got caught up in the drug culture. I heard people would see him a walking around like a zombie, dirty clothes, tangled hair, long beard, and digging through trash dumpsters behind restaurants for food."

"That's awful," John said. "And sad as well."

"He was found under a bridge, overdosed on heroin. Dead to the world. He was only thirty or so."

John's thoughts quickly went to Brody, who had battled opiate addiction for more than a year. He wondered if Stan received any social support during his ordeal or if he had simply been written off as a homeless and hopeless junkie in the seventies.

"I don't remember Stan being like that in school," John said. "Occasionally, we'd drink a beer or two and get a bottle of a cheap fruit wine. That was about it."

"I think he just got in the wrong crowd. You know how it was back then. A lot of folks were experimenting with grass, LSD, coke, and whatever. Most of us survived it and moved on with our lives, but a few couldn't handle it."

"I know," John said with a pensive expression. "Some things haven't changed."

"Aside from that, those were some good times. It was a great time to be growing up."

"At least we thought so."

"Turbulent times, but we were young and ready for most anything."

John stared into the distance. "Or dumb enough to think we were. We were going to live forever."

"Are we bringing up some bad memories?" Virgie asked.

"No, it just got me thinking about some things I haven't thought about in years. Time flies by so quickly it's sometimes hard to believe it was fifty or so years ago. Sometimes it seems like yesterday, and sometimes you wonder if you lived things or simply imagined them."

"I know what you mean, Johnny. Talking about the past alters my mind to some extent. Remember George Harrison said, 'If you remember the 1960s, you weren't there.'"

"I've always tried to focus on the present and future, but as I've gotten older, I seem to think about my fading past."

"One thing I've learned is that life is short, no matter how long you live."

"As one of our friends would say, amen to that."

Fifteen

Sally was in the shower when John returned to the room. He sat on the bed and turned on the TV. It seemed like every channel was showing a football game. He'd already had his fill of football for the day simply being around the Buckeye fans all over the city. The cable news channels were talking heads recounting the slow erosion of democracy, from both ends of the political spectrum, from the previous five days. He finally settled on *The Maltese Falcon*, a film noir starring Humphrey Bogart, on Turner Classic Movies. He propped up the pillow against the headboard, kicked off his shoes, and plopped on the bed.

Sally wasn't in a hurry in the bathroom, making herself pretty, a task that didn't require much effort, he thought. He heard her brushing her teeth, the on-and-off of the water faucet, personal items clanging against the porcelain counter, and the humming of the exhaust fan. She finally stepped out of the room, naked as a jay bird, and walked to her luggage for clean underclothes.

"Well, well, well," John said with a roguish grin. "Look who we have here!"

"Don't get any ideas," she said with a restrained laugh. "You had your chance, mister."

"I know," he said. "I blew it as usual."

"By the way, where did you go?"

John turned off the TV. "I got a little antsy and decided to take a short walk. I saw Virgie at the gift shop and we ended up talking about the old days."

"Enjoy?" she said, slipping on her panties.

"I found out a few more things about classmates, some I had forgotten about."

"That must have been interesting for an inquiring mind."

"It's interesting to find out what happened to certain classmates."

"Good and bad?"

"Yep," John said, nodding. "Things really haven't changed that much when you think about it. And I don't mean fashion, technology, and various kinds of thingamajigs."

Sally sat on the other bed. "You mean people's lives in general?"

"You hit it right on the nose. We still have drug and alcohol problems. Poverty. Homelessness. Wars. Racism. They're only dressed up in a different way. Kind of depressing."

"I think the big difference is that people seem to acknowledge them more nowadays rather than sweep problems under the carpet."

"Now we throw money at the problems and hope they disappear."

"You're depressing me," Sally said, the corners of her mouth drooping.

John sighed. "You and me both."

"Are you going to shower and change clothes?"

"A little later. The dinner isn't for another three hours. I've got plenty of time."

She fastened her bra. "I should have stayed in bed longer."

"You can always get back in."

"I'm sure you'd like that, you silver-tongued devil."

"One of these days you may yearn for that kind of attention and it won't be there."

"What's that supposed to mean?" Sally asked, her brows furrowed. "You won't love me anymore?"

"Hardly. I'll always love you, and you know that. But there could be some physical problem that could change the dynamics of our relationship."

"Dynamics? I've never heard you use that word."

"You know what I mean," he said. "You're just being difficult."

"It's not going to last forever. Have you ever thought about that? I haven't heard about many couples having active sex lives in their eighties."

"We could be the exception."

"Yes, we could, but I wouldn't count on it. The odds aren't in our favor."

"It might if we did it on a regular basis."

"John, we don't even do it on a regular basis now," Sally said. "Maybe once or twice a month."

"That's because we've had lots of stuff going on the past year."

"And who's to say we won't have a lot going on in the coming year? And the year after?"

"Do you have to be so negative?" he asked with a fake scowl.

"I'm just being realistic."

"But I'm usually the realistic one. You've always said that I can be so practical about things. You know, the newspaperman who only sees the cold, hard facts."

"Most of the time, unless it's something you want."

"Oh, you cut me to the quick," he said, placing his hand over his heart.

"Now you're being the drama queen."

"Am I sensing you don't want to go back to bed?"

"It's finally sinking in?" She sat cross-legged on the side of the bed.

"If you insist."

"Honey, I just got out of the shower. I'm clean. I fixed my face. I've brushed my hair. All I have to do before the dinner is get dressed and put on my lipstick. I don't want to start all over. Does that make it any easier to understand?"

"What do you want to do in the meantime?"

"Do we have to be doing something? I can be content reading a book or magazine, or simply talking to you about things. Or watching TV. Haven't you been watching TV?"

"I suppose we can continue talking," he said. "Is there anything you want to discuss?"

"Let me think," she said, placing a hand on her chin like Rodin's *The Thinker* sculpture.

"Now you're trying to be cute."

She gave coquettish grin.

"Now you're sending mixed signals."

"John, why don't you take a short nap? I think you're just getting anxious about tonight. It might help you to relax a little. I brought a couple magazines I can read while you sleep."

"Maybe so." He stood, removed his pants and shirt, and climbed back into bed. "Are you sure you don't want to join me?"

"I'll wake you up in an hour," she said, taking magazines from her travel bag and sitting on a chair.

"How do you expect me to sleep with you there in your sexy underwear?"

"Honey, you've seen me like this for nearly fifty years. Just close your eyes and try to sleep."

In what seemed like ten minutes, but was nearly an hour and a half, John felt a gentle tapping on his bare shoulder. "It's time to get up, sleepyhead," Sally said, bending over and whispering in his ear.

John rubbed his eyes and glanced at the clock radio on the nightstand. "Why did you let me sleep so long?"

"Because you were tired," Sally said. She was wearing a white pearl necklace and a floral-print dress that revealed slight cleavage. "You still have more than an hour to shower and get ready for the dinner."

"You're beautiful," he said, sitting on the side of the bed. "Is that a new dress?"

"It is," she said, taking a mini-bow, holding out the skirt. "I bought it while I was in New York caring after Chloe. It was her idea. She thought I should have a new dress for the reunion."

"You'll be the queen of the ball."

"I want to look nice for you."

"You're gorgeous, and you'll look great to the whole class."

As John slipped out from under the sheet and headed to the bathroom, Sally picked up her cellphone and sat down. "I'm going to call Mother while you're in the shower."

John came out of the bathroom, naked except for rubbing a towel over his thinning hair. Sally had laid out his boxers and socks on the other bed.

"Any news from the home front?" he asked as he pulled up his boxers.

"As usual, I interrupted one of Mother's shows on TV," Sally said with a laugh.

"Heaven forbid."

"Speaking of heaven, Wendell and Libby are attending some kind of religious conference."

"Religious conference? Where?"

"Mother said it was at one of the churches in our neighborhood. It must have been a multi-denominational meeting."

"Just as long as they make periodic checks on your mother."

"She says it's been rather quiet around the house other than a few phone calls."

"Must be someone selling an extended car warranty or Medicare plan," John said with a chuckle. "I'm surprised we haven't received one here."

"Mother did say someone asked where we were, but she wouldn't tell them."

"I hope it wasn't someone important."

"As you'd say, no news is good news."

"That makes me feel better," he said, pulling up his pants. "It always seems like something bad happens when we're away. Let's keep our fingers crossed."

"I'm a little excited about this evening. We don't get dressed up that often. I'm curious about seeing more of your classmates. Are you?"

"Eh, I have mixed feelings. I'll try to make the most of it since we're here. But you know I didn't want to be here to begin with."

"As if you haven't told me a zillion times."

"I just don't want you to forget."

"Hasn't it been nice seeing old friends like Virgie?"

"I have to admit that seeing him is a pleasant surprise. It's funny how you can see someone after fifty years and you practically pick up like it was only yesterday. I wonder why."

"I have a few girlfriends like that. I think it might be the connection we make before we get tied down with becoming adults."

"Personal baggage?"

"You could say that."

"We go on our separate paths that change us in many ways," John said.

"But we share memories with friends from long ago."

"I wonder how things would be if we spent a prolonged period with our old friends? I somehow think we'd learn we don't have a lot in common and would probably drift apart."

"I believe it depends on what you have in common," Sally said. "I have friends that we share our thoughts about parenting, home décor, cooking, health issues, and things like that. We feel comfortable with each other to open up about things that trouble us."

"That's more of a female thing, don't you think? Women are more open about their lives than men are. Guys are too private."

"I won't argue with that. Getting information from you at times is like pulling teeth."

John finished getting dressed, putting on light tan slacks, white shirt, and dark blue blazer. "How do I look?" he asked, posing like a model.

"Aren't you going to wear a tie?"

"I hadn't planned on it. Who wears a tie nowadays? I didn't even bring one with me."

"A tie would have been nice touch, but otherwise, you look handsome. I hope I can keep the women off you."

"Now look who's doing the flattering."

"That reminds me of an old song from the fifties."

"Oh, 'Mutual Admiration Society' from an old Broadway musical, of which I forgot the name."

"That's us," Sally said. "We all need encouragement and support."

"Especially as we grow older."

"People need encouragement at all stages of their lives."

"Spoken like a great teacher," John said.

"We still have thirty minutes before the dinner. When do you think we should leave?"

"In about twenty-nine minutes."

"I don't think so," Sally said.

"What's wrong with being fashionably late?"

"Because that's not who we are. And it's not being considerate to the organizers."

"You're right. We'll leave in twenty minutes."

"More like fifteen."

"If you say so."

"Have you taken your meds?"

"Thanks for reminding me," John said as he walked over to his toiletry pouch and took out two plastic pill containers.

"Maybe you won't be so antsy."

"I'm good." He removed two pills and went to the bathroom to take them with a glass of water.

When he came back, Sally was in front of the mirror touching up lipstick on her puckered mouth. "Let's go," she said, stepping into pastel blue pumps.

They stepped out of their room, noticing several other couples ahead of them going toward a conference room that had been reconfigured for the reunion dinner and dance. As they were about to enter, Sally noticed they had forgotten their nametags.

"Wait here," John said as they stood to the side. "I'll go back and get them."

He dashed back to the room, stopping in the bathroom to urinate, and using her brush to quickly shape his beard, before going back to the reunion room. Sally was talking to three other women, who were also waiting for their husbands to return with nametags.

"That took longer than expected," she said.

"I had some other business to take care of."

They walked into the room, surveyed the tables, and went to one on the side. Paul Mauriat's "Love Is Blue" played softly in the background. Several classmates stood in front of an open bar placing their orders to an overworked bartender and barkeep. A small space had been left open for a dance floor. Purple and gold school colors highlighted the room, from the tablecloths to streamers hanging from the ceiling to flower arrangements to a large banner at the far end reading, "Welcome 50th Reunion, Riley High School Class of 1968."

An unnaturally dark-haired woman wearing a tight-fitting gold-sequined dress came over to John and stared at his nametag, then studied his face before shaking her head and walking away squint-eyed, as if she were confused.

"Do you know her?" Sally asked with an amused expression.

"I guess not, since she apparently didn't recognize me."

"Mind if I sit with you guys?" John turned and saw Virgie approaching the table wearing a black tuxedo.

"Of course," John said.

"Is that a yes or no?" he said with a laugh.

"I think you know the answer. And damn, you're putting me to shame with that outfit."

"Hey, I like to dress up for special occasions, much like your lovely wife."

"Why thank you, Virgie," Sally said with a light blush. "And you're very handsome tonight."

"Let me get us something to drink," John said.

"Red wine for me," Sally said.

"Same here," Virgie said.

"Won't be the same for me," John said. "I'm getting a beer."

"I wonder if they still sell Hudepohl?" Virgie asked. "We drank a lot of three-point-two Hudys back in the day."

"Getting moody with Hudy," John said.

"That and Burger beer."

"Some good times, my friend."

John walked over to the bar while Sally and Virgie sat at the table. Most of the classmates and their spouses or significant others were milling about the room. There were several tables with yearbooks. Someone had put together several large collages with headlines, photographs, and stories from the local and school newspapers. A small table in the corner illuminated by a single candle displayed photos of the deceased.

John made it back to the table, spilling some beer on his hand along the way. He handed glasses of wine to Sally and Virgie.

"Virgie told me a few interesting stories about you," Sally said, as John sat between them.

"You better consider your source. Some are unreliable, especially after fifty years." He gently nudged Virgie. "Beware of fake news."

"More of that newspaper talk," Sally said. "Anyway, I didn't know you were in a band."

"Like I said, consider your source. We were a poor excuse for a band."

"We were the Beats," Virgie said with a laugh.

"A rip-off of the Beatles?" Sally asked.

"Yes and no," Virgie said. "We wanted to be like the Beatles, but we got our name from the Beat poets. Remember Allen Ginsberg, Jack Kerouac, William S. Burroughs, and those writers?"

"That sounds plausible."

"Believe it or not, we weren't good," John said. "I think we lasted about six months, if that long."

"I believe you," Sally said. "I've heard you sing in the shower."

"Thanks a lot."

"Our repertoire consisted of about fifteen songs we played over and over. Mostly Beach Boys, Tommy James, and Beatles. Nothing original from us," Virgie said.

Seconds later, Tommy James and the Shondells' "Mony Mony" played on the sound system. "We didn't sound anything like that," John said.

"We were ahead of our time."

"You think?"

"Oh sure, with the loud punk bands a decade later, we would have fit right in."

"I'm not so sure about that," John said. "We were loud, but that's about it."

"Oh, well, it's a nice thought."

"I'm going to ask you something, and I want you to tell me the truth," John said. "Have you told any of your arsty-fartsy friends out west that you were in a garage band like The Stooges or Blue Cheer?"

Virgie burst out laughing. "I haven't, but I will now."

Sixteen

"You'd think they'd play that song after dinner," Virgie said, as "Mony, Mony" wound down.

"They probably got a mix of music from sixty-eight," John said. "I wouldn't be surprised to hear "Born to Be Wild" while we eat."

"Now be honest, John, you listen to these songs regardless of the time of day or the occasion," Sally said.

"But I was a kid. I'm an old geezer now. I prefer soft rock later in the day."

"Oh, come on Johnny, admit it, you're an oldie but goodie," Virgie said.

"Maybe a moldy oldie."

"You'll be an old geezer if you think that way," Virgie said. "Remember, you're only as old as you think you are."

"How about how I feel?"

"You can feel physically old and be mentally young. It's all a matter of attitude," Sally said. "Studies show those with positive attitudes live longer."

"Phooey," John said with a mischievous grin, "Sounds like false news to me."

"Just Google it."

"You're right, Sally," Virgie said with a smile. "My thoughts exactly."

"I give up," John said with a grin. "I'm outnumbered. You guys win."

"Now that's a good sign," Virgie said. "You're showing flexibility in your thinking rather than being set in your ways. There's still hope for you, Johnny."

"Whew," John said, wiping a hand over his forehead. "I'm not over the hill yet."

Virgie laughed. "Heading that way, but not over the top."

"You folks mind if we join you?" a balding man with long sideburns asked from the opposite end of the round table.

"Please do," John said, rising slightly from his chair while trying to read the man's nametag.

"Robert Potts," the man said in a rasping voice. "You probably remember me as Bobby Joe. My wife, Agnes." She had a cherubic face and curly salt-and-pepper hair dangling to her shoulders.

John's eyes widened, trying to connect the name with the face. The Bobby Joe he remembered was short and skinny. The classmate before him was tall and overweight.

"It's been a long time," John said, flashing a grin.

"At least a half century," Bobby Joe said, as he pulled out a chair for his wife. "I must admit you folks have changed a bit. Is that your daughter?"

"More like my queen," John said, smiling, placing a hand over Sally's.

"One thing I can say about your classmates is they know how to flatter the gals," Sally said.

"And guys, too," Bobby Joe, glancing at Virgie. "You're a standout in the tuxedo."

John sensed Virgie tensing up at the comment. "We had our share, didn't we?" he said, patting Virgie on the shoulder.

"What have you been up to all these years?" Virgie asked Bobby Joe.

"Got my plumber's license a couple years after high school and stayed with it. Started my own company and passed it on to my sons. BJ and Sons."

"BJ?" Virgie asked, scrunching his brows.

"Bobby Joe. What do you think?"

"Uh, never mind."

John and Virgie gave Bobby Joe a rundown of their activities since high school.

"You guys still working?"

"Staying busy, but not drawing a paycheck," John said. "Trying to enjoy retirement as much as I can. I'm hoping it'll last quite a few years."

"An artist never retires," Virgie said. "I've always got some project going on."

"Sweetie and I bought a little place south of Panama City," Bobby Joe said. "We'll be heading down there in November and come back in March. And if the weather's bad, we'll stay a little longer."

"Into golf?" John asked.

"Hell no. Never had time for that silly game. I spend most of my time deep-water fishing with a few other snowbirds I met down there."

"How about you, Agnes?" Sally asked.

"I just tag along with Bobby Joe, when he lets me," she said, with an anxious smile. "Most times, I stay around the house and babysit the grandkids."

"That keeps her busy," Bobby Joe said. "We got eleven and probably some more on the way."

"Any daughters?" Sally asked.

"Thank God, no! They wouldn't have been much help with the plumbing business."

"I see."

"We do have three granddaughters," Agnes said with a bashful smile.

The Grass Roots' "Midnight Confession" played while one of the organizers flicked the lights, signaling it was time to be seated at a table. Shortly thereafter, the wait staff brought garden salads and set them before the attendees.

"That's some mighty slim pickins," Bobby Joe said, raising his brows. "I hope the main course is better. A man could starve around here."

The others remained silent as the waiters returned and asked for their drink orders. Penelope Byers, one of the organizers, stepped up to the lectern and tapped on the microphone several times before speaking. "I just want to welcome and thank everyone for attending our fiftieth reunion. We'll eat, then break to give everybody some time to go around and talk to friends and classmates. We end with a dance with music provided by a DJ. I hope each person has a wonderful evening. And don't forget, tomorrow we meet once again for a picnic and games. Enjoy!"

"Hold it a minute, Penny," came a voice from the middle of the room. Everyone watched as Tyrone Brune made his way to the lectern.

"Forgive me, Tyrone," she said. "I got in a hurry and forgot about the benediction."

Tyrone solemnly stood before the gathering, a faint smile beginning to spread on his face. "Bow with me, please," he intoned. "Our gracious heavenly Father, we thank you for giving us this great occasion for our brothers and sisters in Christ to congregate for this class reunion. We are truly thankful for all you have bestowed upon us in the fifty years that have passed since we graduated from Riley High School."

There was an "amen" from one of the tables. John assumed it was from Maggie, Tyrone's devout spouse.

"Thank you, dear Lord, for giving us safe travels here. And we pray that you will provide us again with safe travels to our humble abodes. We ask you bless those that organized this reunion of souls. We are eternally grateful for all you do for us."

"Amen!"

"We ask you bless the hands that prepared our meals," Tyrone continued, "and the nourishment it provides. More than anything, we thank you, God, for sending us your Son and the promise of everlasting life. In your holy name we pray. Amen."

"Amen and praise the Lord!

"Amen," several others uttered as Tyrone returned to his table.

"I never knew Tyrone had become a preacher man," Bobby Joe said. "I figured he'd end up in prison. He was a dang good basketball player, but that's about it."

"He went to Iowa on a basketball scholarship and played pro ball for several years before pursing the ministry," John said. "He's led a good life, working with the disadvantaged in Chicago."

"Those welfare queens and druggies?"

"Don't you think they've done a wonderful job setting this up?" Sally said, interrupting the course of the conversation.

"A little pricey, if you're asking me," Bobby Joe said. "We almost decided not to come."

"Why's that?" John asked.

"I know a lot of the people here. I see them every blue moon at the zoo, football games, or some other thing around town. Even did plumbing in some of their homes. Would you believe they wanted discounts?"

"What about those who don't live here?" Virgie asked.

"That was kind of the tipping point for me. Since it's a one-time deal, I figured there'd be a few guys I'd like to see. Like you, John."

"It's been great so far, reconnecting with Virgie and others," John said, nodding to his friend. "We've shared a lot of memories since we got here yesterday."

"Probably many more that we've forgotten," Virgie said.

"I'm glad you decided to attend," John said to Bobby Joe as he lightly bumped his knee against Sally's. "Our paths may never cross again."

"Ever make it back to Columbus?"

"Other than my parents' funerals, this is the first time."

"So it's likely this will be the last time," Bobby Joe said with a chuckle.

"I've returned a few times," Virgie said. "But it's been a while since my last visit."

"Oh."

As Cream's "Sunshine of Your Love" played, the waiters began removing the salad dishes and putting main course plates with roast beef, mashed potatoes, and carrots on the tables.

"You've got to be kidding me," Bobby Joe said. "We paid a hundred dollars for this? This is something they'd served on the lunchroom line back in high school."

"Brings back more memories," Virgie said with a grin. "Yummy."

"You can't be serious," Bobby Joe said indignantly. "They could have offered chicken or fish."

"I didn't come here for the meal," John said. "More for the fellowship with old friends."

"I may have to stop at McDonald's on the way home," Bobby Joe said. "This is pitiful."

"Don't forget there's a picnic tomorrow," Virgie said. "When you figure in the cocktail social last night, the golf scramble, tonight's activities, and the Sunday get-together, it's quite a bargain."

"And more so for you, since you and Agnes can stay at your home instead of the motel," John said.

"You couldn't pay me to stay at this dump," Bobby Joe said. "I've done some jobs here and this place sucks. Mold everywhere. I've seen rats as large as cats. Disgusting."

"Really?" John asked, tilting his head. "I thought our room was clean. The motel is rather outdated, but the upkeep seems good."

"Kind of nostalgic," Virgie said. "A throwback to the seventies. Even charming in an odd way."

"It was built after you guys left Columbus," Bobby Joe said. "It must be forty-five years old."

"Oh, it's still part of the era," Virgie said. "Kinda historic, in a sense."

"I can see that," John agreed.

"I hope they got rid of the roach problem," Bobby Joe said. "The health department had them under notice for quite a while."

"Thanks for sharing," John said, glancing at his food. "How long ago was that?"

"About twenty years."

"I think we should be in the clear then," Virgie said.

"I'm gonna get me another beer," Bobby Joe said, rising from his chair. He walked away without asking the others if they wanted something from the bar.

"Please forgive Bobby Joe," Agnes said, just above a whisper. "He hasn't been feeling well lately."

"I hope it's not anything serious," John said.

"It's nothing physical. He's upset with all the politics going on. He gets so worked up watching news on TV. I try to get him to turn it off, but he won't. He loves his country so much and hates to see where it's headed."

"Oh," John said, nodding.

"Where is it headed?" Virgie said, drawing his head back.

"You know, socialism and abortions," she said. "Please don't bring any of that up when he gets back."

"How about guns?"

"Bobby Joe's has mixed feelings about that. A neighbor shot and killed one of our dogs a few years back, and he hasn't gotten over it."

"Does he own a gun?" John asked.

"He used to carry one in his truck in case he went into colored neighborhoods. I guess he still has it. I haven't asked him."

"Ignorance is bliss," Virgie said, shaking his head.

"Please don't mention any of this to him," Agnes said. "I don't want to see him get upset."

"We'll try to remember that," John said as he watched Bobby Joe shuffle his way back to the table, patting several guys on the back along the way.

"Most certainly," Virgie said.

"My ears are burning," Bobby Joe said as he sat down. "You guys been talking about me?"

John noticed Agnes stiffen in her chair.

"You have good ears," he said. "Agnes was telling us how successful you've been with your company. We're impressed."

A smile eased across Agnes' tense face.

"She's a big reason for it," Bobby Joe, putting an arm around her shoulders. "She handles the books."

"So you haven't retired yet?" Sally asked Agnes.

"I've cut back some, and I'm trying to teach the books to one of our daughters-in-law," Agnes said. "It takes time."

"Our boys didn't marry the brightest gals," Bobby Joe said. "They're good at making babies, but that's about it. They don't show much ambition."

"Maybe you can hire an accounting firm," Virgie said. "I use one for my business."

"No way, Josè. Agnes here saves us a ton of money. I don't want someone out of the family prying into my financial affairs."

"I see," Virgie said, nodding.

"Are you from around here, Agnes?" Sally asked.

"I was a couple years behind Bobby Joe," she said. "I was in the class of seventy."

"How did you meet Bobby Joe?"

"He was a friend of my older brother, Leroy," she said, glancing at Bobby Joe as if seeking approval to speak. "Leroy was already a plumber, and Bobby Joe did his apprenticeship under him. Right, Bobby Joe?"

"Enough about Agnes. Guess who I saw at the bar?" Bobby Joe said.

"I give up," John said.

"Grover Jones," Bobby Joe said with a wide grin. "I see him around town at times, but wasn't sure he'd be here. He's a fun guy."

"I guess it depends on a person's idea of fun," Virgie said.

"Grover talks big, but he's a puppy at heart. He likes to have fun with people. I don't pay him no mind."

"He didn't pick on you in high school?" John asked.

"Hell, I think he picked on most anybody. I was a little feller back then, so I was smart enough to keep my distance. Things changed when I finally started filling out."

"I see," Virgie said.

"Now he's getting a little shit-faced over there," Bobby Joe said. "It should be a fun night."

"I'm sure."

Seventeen

The waitstaff brought slices of chocolate cake to the tables and retrieved the main course of those who had finished their meals. The Box Tops' "Cry Like a Baby" played in the background.

"Finally, something that's decent to eat," Bobby Joe said, eyeing the piece of cake. He swallowed a bite. "Not bad. I've had better, but this isn't bad. Not bad at all."

"I'm going to get another beer," John said as he rose from his chair. "Can I get anyone something to drink?"

"I'm good," Sally said.

"Nothing for me, but thank you for asking," Agnes said politely.

"I'll take another glass of red wine," Virgie said.

"Hey, bud, since you're going, you might as well get me another beer," Bobby Joe said. "By the way, are you going to eat your cake?"

"Well, uh, you can have it," John said. "Chocolate doesn't mix well with beer."

"Maybe not for you," Bobby Joe said, as he reached halfway over the table for John's slice instead of asking for it to be passed to him.

"I guess that means you can't have your cake and eat it too," Virgie said.

"Good one," Sally said with a bright smile.

As John stood at the bar, a man came up from behind and patted him on the back. "Hi, stranger."

John turned, peered at the nametag, and said, "It's been a long time, Reggie. Great to see you." Reggie, tall with a thick shock of white hair and a short ponytail, vigorously shook his hand to the point it almost felt like his arm might become disconnected.

"I saw your name on the registration list, but had trouble picking you out," Reggie said. "You had peach fuzz on your face back then. I'd also say you were somewhat lighter."

"I think most of us were back then," John said as they stepped to the side of the bar.

John gave him a condensed version of his history since high school. "I heard you were a sportswriter but couldn't find your byline," Reggie said. "Were you a stringer or something like that?"

"No, I was a sportswriter and became a sports editor in Lexington. I didn't have many bylines near the end of my career because I spent more time managing the pages than writing columns and stories. But they're out there on the Internet if you're interested in reading them."

"I'll have to do that," Reggie said. "You know, I never figured you for a sportswriter. When I heard about it, it surprised the hell out of me. You didn't seem like the sports type in high school, if you know what I mean."

John glanced back the table and noticed Bobby Joe turned around as if wondering what was taking him so long.

"I'm sure I surprised a few people. Even myself. But I did write for the school paper."

"Really? I suppose I read your little articles."

"A lot of folks didn't."

"Uh, well it's great seeing you. Let's chat later or tomorrow, if we bump into each other."

"Sounds like a plan," John said as he picked up his drinks from the counter. "Enjoy the evening."

"You were gone long enough," Bobby Joe said when John returned to the table. "Who were you gabbing with?"

"Reggie Tillman."

"I remember him," Virgie said. "Wasn't he senior class president or something like that?"

"I believe so," John said. "I wonder if he went into politics."

"If he did, it wasn't around here," Bobby Joe said. "Didn't you ask him what he was doing now?"

"I didn't have time," John said with a light chuckle. "I had your beer order to take care of."

"And Virgil's wine. It just wasn't me."

Penny returned to the lectern, telling the group there would be thirty minutes of social time before the dance.

"I guess we should get up and socialize with our classmates," John said.

"I'm not sure thirty minutes will be long enough," Virgie said. "Especially if we come across some long-winded folks."

"As long as they keep the music at a decent level, it shouldn't be a problem talking during the dance. I know I didn't come all this way to dance."

"You've got that right, Johnny," Bobby Joe said. "That was a stupid idea."

"Some people like to dance," Virgie said.

"I still think it's a stupid idea."

John rose from the table, tapping Sally on the back. "Let's move about and see who's here. Or better yet, see if I recognize anyone."

"Or if they recognize you," Sally said.

"I think I'll do the same," Virgie said. "I saw a few familiar faces." He headed toward the tables at the front of the room.

"We're going to stay here for a while," Bobby Joe said. "Maybe later." Agnes sat rigidly in her chair, sad-faced like an abandoned kitten.

Sally removed the camera from her purse and aimed it at Bobby Joe and Agnes. "Smile." A second later, a befuddled look emerged on Bobby Joe's face and a timorous one on Agnes' before the camera's flash. The couple glanced at each other, stone-faced, as if stunned that someone would want a photo of them.

"I hope we didn't break your camera," Bobby Joe exclaimed.

"You guys look wonderful," Sally said with a warm smile. "Especially Agnes. I love your dress."

Agnes lowered her head slightly as if examining her attire, a pastel green dress with ruffled shoulders and lace bodice revealing modest cleavage. "Thank you," she said softly.

John and Sally maneuvered among several tables as he glimpsed at the faces. Others began to move around the room while the Classic IV's "Spooky" filled the space. John glanced back at Bobby Joe and Agnes, sitting stiffly at the table with somber expressions.

"You're going shoot me for saying this, but Bobby Joe is a lot like you in a bad way," Sally said.

"What?" John said, stopping abruptly.

"He's kind of grumpy."

"So you're telling me I'm grumpy like him?"

"Well, you're more of a lovable curmudgeon," she said. "That's a big difference."

"Gee, thanks."

"Do you see anyone you know?" she asked as they resumed ambling among the attendees.

"This is more difficult than I thought it would be," John said. "They probably should have gone around and had each person identify themselves."

At that moment, a woman tugged at John's coat sleeve. "Remember me?" she asked with bright eyes.

"Uh..."

"Diane Rinaldi. Well, I was Diane West in high school."

"Oh, Diane," John said, taking a step back to get a full view of her petite frame, regal nose, and silvery hair. "It's good to see you, and this is my wife Sally."

Giving a little nod to Sally, Diane asked with a doe-eyed expression, "Where have all the years gone?"

"Not far from you," he said. "You look great."

"You do as well, John."

John turned toward Sally. "Diane lived down the street from me. We first met in elementary school."

"That's right, John," Diane said. "It was Mrs. Goble's third-grade class. My family had just moved into the neighborhood. John was like a brother. He always watched out for me. That's something I never forgot. You married a knight in shining armor."

Sally looked at John with a warm smile. "I think so, too."

"You gals are embarrassing me," John said with a light blush. "Where is your knight in shining armor, Diane? I'd like to meet him."

"Oliver passed three years ago," she said, pursing her lips.

"Oh, I'm so sorry. Was he a classmate?"

"We met a few years after I graduated from Oberlin. We worked at the same architectural firm in Buffalo, New York. We had three wonderful children, and then seven beautiful grandchildren. He developed liver cancer and lived for about two years before he died. But we had a good life together. I still miss him so." Her eyes watered.

"He does sound like a knight in shining armor," Sally said sympathetically.

"John, do you remember that time in middle school when those awful boys pushed me in a corner and tried to touch me all over? You came to my rescue and pulled them away from me."

"I wasn't going to let them do anything to you. You were one of my best friends."

"But there were some other boys who just stood there and watched."

"I don't know what to say," he said. "I wasn't going to let anyone hurt you."

"Your actions spoke louder than words back then."

"Enough about me. Do you still live in Buffalo?"

"I moved to the Pittsburgh area to be closer to my children. I live in a senior living village that's extremely convenient and safe. And you?"

"We're in Lexington," John said. "I got into the newspaper business and spent most of my career there."

"I was going to ask if you ever wrote that novel. Sally, he confided in me that one day he was going to be a novelist. I always wondered if that happened. You had such a way with words, John."

"I never wrote that novel," John said, with a slight shrug. "I got too busy with other things in life. And spending so much time as a newspaperman, I think it gradually drained the words out of me, if that makes any sense."

"Maybe you can go back to it after a few years and get recharged," Diane said. "Retirement does take some getting used to."

"That could happen. You never know."

"I suppose I should circulate some more. I hope you'll be at the picnic tomorrow."

"We plan to be there," John said. "By the way, if you're around here later, maybe save a dance for me?"

"Only if it's okay with Sally," Diane said with a sparkle in her eyes. "I don't want to steal her knight in shining armor."

"I think I'll be fine for one dance," Sally said, smiling.

Diane hugged them both, said a quick goodbye and went to another table.

"What a sweet woman," Sally said.

"She was smart, too," John said. "She helped me get through some math courses. I'm not surprised she got involved in architecture."

"Was she your first girlfriend?"

"I suppose so, in a platonic sense. You remember her saying I was like a brother to her."

Richard Harris's "MacArthur Park" played in the background as John, holding Sally's hand, strolled toward several people at one of the collages. A couple turned around and faced them for a couple seconds before flashing knowing grins.

"If it isn't Mr. John Ross, my revolutionary friend of the sixties," the man exclaimed, drawing attention to those standing nearby. "Are you still marching for all the causes, great and small?"

"That was a long time ago, Mr. Wayne White," John said with a wide smile. "How about you? Still carrying the torch of freedom?"

They shook hands before John realized the woman with Wayne was Martha Asher, another classmate. John held her hand for a few seconds before introducing Sally to his old classmates.

Sally got them to pause for a few seconds as she took a photo of the trio, Martha in the middle, her arms around each guy's waist.

"You still look like you could get involved in a protest march," Wayne said. "At least with that beard. Not so sure about the hair, unless you grew a ponytail."

John motioned them over to a vacant table. "Let's sit and catch up on some things."

"Remember that time we skipped school and participated in that Martin Luther King march in Cincinnati?" said Wayne, his slick-backed hair and Armani suit giving him a silver fox image, a vast departure from his days as a scruffy counter-culture activist. "And then we tried to start something the next day at school and nearly got suspended?"

"You could say we were rebels without a cause, especially in the eyes of Principal Edwards. We almost didn't graduate that year."

"Didn't you go with us to Cincinnati?" John asked Martha, who hadn't changed much over the years, thanks to specific cosmetic surgery on her neck and face. Her hair was still blonde, though a bit dull, but her blue eyes glimmered, no doubt because of contacts.

"I didn't make that trip," she said. "But I did sneak off with you guys and go to a Vietnam War protest on the OSU campus."

"I seem to recall we had bold plans to go to Chicago for the Democratic National Convention but that was nixed when Bobby Kennedy was assassinated that summer," Wayne said.

"It was a pipe dream from a couple teenagers," John said. "It sounded cool around our friends, but we didn't have hardly a penny to our names. I know my parents wouldn't have given it to me."

"Shoot, we couldn't even vote back then," Wayne said with a laugh.

"Are you guys together?" John asked.

"Only for the weekend," Wayne said softly. "My wife is back in Denver."

"And my husband is in Boston," Martha whispered.

John and Sally looked at each other. "Maybe I should have stayed at home," she said with a crinkly grin.

"I don't think so," John said, putting an arm around her waist.

"Don't do as we do," Martha said, with a guilt-ridden expression. "But we go back a long way. Wayne and I dated through high school and in college. Then we went our separate ways."

"What happened?" John asked. "I always figured you guys would marry and live happily ever after."

"Like you and Sally?"

"Yeah, something like that," John said.

"Well, we had some philosophical differences," Martha said. "I joined the Peace Corps, and Wayne got involved in Wall Street."

"That's about it," Wayne said. "She went after spiritual fulfillment, and I sought the golden calf."

John opened his eyes wide. "Wow. That's quite a difference. I would have never guessed that, especially for you, Wayne."

"I made several million in hedge funds and moved to Denver," Wayne said. "I love skiing so I also have a chalet near Aspen. You and Sally need to visit sometime. I'd love for you to meet Vivian."

"Vivian?"

"My wife," Wayne said. "She's number four, but who's counting." He laughed mildly.

"What about you, Martha?" John asked.

"I met Jerome while I was working in Peru in the late seventies. We got married and then moved around quite a bit as he got involved as a political consultant."

"Democrat?"

"That's what most people would assume, but he got caught up

in Reagan and has become an arch-conservative. Some would say he's part of a cult. It kinda freaks me out at times."

"You as well?"

"I'm a closet Democrat, but that's our secret. We don't have a lot in common anymore, other than two children and five grands," she said. "He goes to all the Republican activities, while I generally stay in Boston and spend my time at art shows, book festivals, and such. I guess I evolved into a social butterfly. Who would have guessed?" She laughed.

"Pardon me for being nosy, but how did you guys connect?" John asked.

"Ah, the curious news reporter," Wayne said, raising his brows. "Always seeking the truth."

"Jerome had a political retreat in Aspen, and I decided to go with him," Martha said. "We'd skied some in New Hampshire and Vermont, so I thought it would be fun to try the slopes in Colorado."

"And who does she see at the lodge?" Wayne said with a wide grin. "*Moi!*"

"Jerome was in a meeting, so Wayne and I went to the bar and talked and talked and talked," Martha said. "This was about ten years ago."

"Martha would notify me where she and Jerome would be going every year, and I'd make arrangements to be there as well," Wayne said. "Her hubby would be in meetings for hours on end, allowing us to be together. It's worked out well."

"Your wife doesn't suspect anything?" Sally asked Wayne.

"She's highly active in little civic activities. I think she likes it when I'm away. I'm not under her feet."

"Maybe she's having fun on her own."

"Oh, you naughty lady," Wayne said, wagging his finger at her. "But that would be hilarious. If only you knew Vivian."

"Maybe I will someday, if John and I accept your invitation to visit."

Wayne gave a pensive pose before laughing. "It's an open invitation."

"What about you, John?" Martha asked. "Didn't you go to college in Kentucky?"

"I got a journalism degree at Eastern Kentucky, then went into the military for a couple years. It's been newspapers since then."

"I'm surprised you went in the military after your rebel-rousing days," Wayne said. "What brought that on?"

"I wasn't going to Canada, or even be a conscientious objector, although some friends tried to persuade me to do that," John said. "And thinking back on it, they didn't either. Some lucked out with the draft, and some didn't. But my dad was a veteran and several of my relatives served during World War Two and the Korean War. I guess it was a family tradition that I couldn't dishonor. Does that make sense?"

"It does to me," Wayne said. 'It would have been difficult for me, even though I hated the Vietnam War and all it represented. My father was in World War Two. I even had an uncle who died in the Pacific theater by the Japanese. The sixties were difficult and confusing times for youngsters."

"At least we survived it all, for better or for worse."

Eighteen

The overhead lights flickered several times, then the DJ shouted that it was time for folks to put on their dancing shoes. Moments later, Sly and the Family Stone's "Dance to the Music" filled the room. Many couples looked at each other and sat at the nearest tables, preferring to rest their tired or swollen feet than boogie on the dance floor.

"I'm almost tempted to go back to our room," John said to Sally, leaning toward her to make sure he was heard over the pounding music.

"How about going to the bar?" Wayne asked. "It certainly can't be as loud as this."

"I hate to leave after all the effort some folks put into this. Maybe we can get the music man to turn it down a few decibels."

John glanced at the exit and noticed several couples leaving. Four couples were on the dance floor, robotically moving to the beat of the tune. He wondered if their joints were creaking as well.

Virgie came over, followed by classmate Cindy Maxwell, her gray hair teased high on her head, a throwback to when a bouffant was popular, and wearing a blue-sequined mini-dress and net stockings.

"Mind if we join you guys?" Virgie asked. "I assume everyone remembers Cindy." She flashed a batty-eyed smile, precariously holding a tall drink that may have been one of too many.

"Hi Cindy," John said. "I'm not sure if I'd recognize you outside of here."

"I love your outfit," Sally said, introducing herself with a handshake.

"I hope I didn't dress too trashy," she said. "I wanted to get into the spirit of the reunion."

"We all probably should have done that," John said. "Make it more of a costume party."

"That means we probably would have worn bell bottoms, tie-dyed T-shirts, and sandals," Virgie said, grinning. "I had plenty of those back in the day."

"The women may have dressed up in granny dresses and beads," Martha said.

"Or maybe those sexy mini-skirts," Wayne chimed in.

"Don't forget peace-symbol necklaces," Sally said.

"I had a ring with a peace symbol on it," John said. "I think I lost it in boot camp."

Steppenwolf's "Born to Be Wild" blared through the speakers. John excused himself and walked over to the DJ's booth. The young man nodded with an OK salute. Seconds later, the decibels dropped a few notches as John reached the table.

"Thanks for taking care of that," Wayne said. "I thought I was going to have to remove my hearing aids."

"If you're like me, you suffered hearing loss from listening to music played too loud at concerts," John said. "Even those turntables from Sears."

"You're right about that. I still enjoy music, but not loud."

"I can hardly listen to the heavy metal I loved. I couldn't get enough of Led Zeppelin, Cream, and Black Sabbath back then."

"Same here," Virgie said. "Now I prefer the softer stuff, like America, Air Supply, and the Carpenters."

"But I'll always listen to the Moody Blues," John said. "The soundtrack of my life."

"The Beatles for me," Wayne said.

"I prefer David Bowie," Virgie said.

"Joni Mitchell for me," Martha said.

"Give me Bruce Springsteen," Sally said.

"I don't care for any of that music anymore," Cindy said. "I like country."

They glared at her with shocked expressions, then broke out laughing.

"Just having fun with you," John said. "Country has become my guilty pleasure."

"I even like rap," Virgie said.

That admission was greeted with bewildered faces.

"Really?" John asked.

"Well, some of it," Virgie said. "I think every music genre has some good stuff."

"You know what they call country when mixed with rap?" Wayne asked the group.

"Wayne, that is so old that it makes you sound old," Martha said, poking him in the side.

"I am old," he said. "So just shoot me."

"There you go," Martha said, shaking her head.

"I'm finished, so stick a fork in me."

"Please, Wayne, take your comedy show to the old folks' home," John said.

"You're killing us with your humor," Virgie said.

"Well, it sure beats some other ways to die," Wayne said.

"Has anyone seen Benji Walton?" John asked. "I thought for sure he'd be here."

"I heard he has Parkinson's disease. Maybe that's the reason."

"Wasn't Benji the prom king?" Martha asked.

"I believe so," Virgie said. "I forgot who the prom queen was."

"I think it was Penelope," Cindy said.

"I believe you're right," Martha said.

"I seem to recall it caused a bit of controversy," Wayne said. "Some people in the school administration and the parent-teacher group were against it because they didn't like the idea of a Black king and white queen. For a while, they were going to strip them of the titles."

"How could I not remember that?" John said. "Wayne, Martha and I started a mini-protest at the school that attracted some media attention. Mr. Edwards backed off after that. The only thing is that the school downplayed the event and didn't make a big deal of it."

"Speaking of the prom, who was your date?" Virgie asked.

"Let me think," John said, lowering his eyes. "It was Meg Rutherford. That was the only time I ever went out with her."

"I remember her," Martha said. "She was part of our little group of misfits and outcasts."

"I went with Barb Collins," Virgie said. "She was in my art class. We didn't have fun."

"And I escorted the lovely and talented Martha Asher," Wayne said, placing his arm around her shoulders.

"How about you, Cindy?" Virgie asked.

"I didn't go," she said, shrugging. "No one asked me."

"Well, you didn't miss much," Wayne said. "The whole thing was a big flop."

"I suppose so," Cindy said, "But it was kinda painful for a seventeen-year-old. There were a few other girls who weren't asked."

"That sucks," Virgie said. "No one should be excluded from a school program."

"That's ages ago and I'm long over it," she said. "But it sure hurt at the time."

Sergio Mendes's "The Look of Love" filled the room, prompting several couples to head to the dance floor.

"May I have this dance?" John asked Sally, taking her hand.

"This is more our speed," she said to the others as they stepped away to dance. Wayne and Martha and then Virgie and Cindy followed them to what became a crowded area with a few butt bumps.

"I didn't care for this song when it came out," John said. "Now it's one of my favorites. It's funny how time can change how you hear things."

"Maybe a change in mindset?"

"No doubt. I wasn't in love with anyone back then, so it didn't connect. But I am now."

"You say the sweetest things," Sally said, resting her head on his shoulder as they swayed to the music.

When the song ended, the DJ apparently sensed what the people wanted to hear and played Willie Mitchell's "Soul Serenade." He followed with Blue Cheer's "Summertime Blues," which practically cleared the floor except for two couples who somehow had the vitality to dance on to the thunderous beat.

"How about one more drink before we call it a night?" John asked. "A nightcap, so to speak, for the old folks."

"John, you're beginning to make me feel old," Wayne said. "Hell, we're only sixty-seven or sixty-eight, unless some folks are lying about their ages. We still have a lot of life in us. At least I hope we do."

"You're right," John said, shrugging. "I'm still trying to get my footing after retiring last year. I need to get back into a groove."

"It's a matter of attitude," Martha said. "You need to have positive thoughts."

"John still has too much newspaper ink in his blood," Sally said. "He still sees too much in black and white."

"Hey, you're supposed to be on my side," John said. "And for the record, I simply try to see things as they are. I don't try to paint a rosy picture about life. Some call me a realist."

John asked the others what they wanted to drink and headed to the bar. "Let me give you a hand," Virgie said as he stood and followed him. Several clusters of classmates were spread in different areas of the room, much like the cliques in high school. John thought some things hadn't changed.

"Having a good time?" John asked Virgie as they waited for the barkeep to complete their order.

"It's been better than I thought it would be."

"Any plans with Cindy?"

"What do you mean?"

"After the dance."

"I think she's going back to her home. She lives on the northside."

"I thought perhaps she was staying here."

"I think you're insinuating something else, but that's okay," Virgie said. "I have no intentions of shacking up with her. We weren't even friends in high school...more like acquaintances."

"I hardly remember her either."

"She came by herself and kinda tagged along after me."

"What has she done since high school?"

"I haven't a clue. You'll have to ask her."

"Okay."

The barkeep put their drinks on two trays. John pulled a ten-dollar bill from his pocket and stuffed it in the tip jar. Gary Lewis and the Playboys' "Sealed with a Kiss" came on as several couples returned to the dance floor.

Before John could sit, Penny came up behind him and tapped him on the shoulder. "Do you mind if I have a dance with your handsome husband?" she asked Sally.

"Go ahead," Sally said, with friendly smile. "Just watch your toes."

"Hey, I resemble that remark!" John said.

Penny led John to the dance floor, holding one hand while John awkwardly placed a hand on her back. "I should warn you that I do have two left feet," he said with a chuckle.

"Your wife warned me."

"She speaks the truth."

"Do you remember when we danced at the junior prom?"

"Uh, I danced with several girls. I think I went stag with some other guys that year."

"Me and some of my friends didn't have dates either," she said. "So we all ended up dancing with lots of guys. It was a lot of fun."

"If you say so. I don't remember some of those dances."

"Did you know I had a crush on you?"

"Uh, I never picked up on that."

"Yes, I always wanted you to ask me out, but you never did." The corners of her mouth turned downward.

"I'm sure you survived my naïve ways. I don't recall having any steady girlfriends back then. In fact, I know I didn't."

"But you remember the parties?"

"A few of them."

"The kissing parties?"

"That was so long ago. Weren't we freshmen and sophomores or junior high?"

"That's right," she said. "You were so cute and bashful."

John chuckled. "Now I'm old and bashful."

"If your wife wasn't sitting over there, I'd be tempted to kiss you again."

"What?" John loosened his hold on her.

"Oh, don't worry, I'm not going to," she said with a giggle. "You can relax.'

"Where is your husband?"

"Greg is at home," she said. "He's been to a few reunions and got bored. He felt it wasn't fun for me because it seemed I felt obliged to entertain him instead of reconnecting with friends. So he goes alone to his reunions, and I do the same now."

"That seems reasonable."

"Maybe you can do that when we have another reunion."

"I'll give it some thought," John said, "but I think Sally likes meeting my former classmates."

"That's a shame."

The song ended and John led her off the floor and back to the table. "Thank you for lending me your husband for a dance," Penny said. "He still has the moves."

John blushed. "I hope I didn't step on your toes."

"You did just fine, Johnny." She pecked him on the cheek. "Too-da-loo!"

"She seemed to enjoy it," Sally said after Penny walked away with a little spring in her step.

"I'm glad someone did."

Sally held out the camera and showed John the photo she had taken of him and Penny on the dance floor.

"You didn't have to do that," he said.

"You mind if I dance with your lovely lady?"

Grover Jones stood next to them, looking at John while holding his hand out for Sally.

"Just be sure and bring her back," John said, as Sally hesitantly stood as Gary Puckett and the Union Gap's "Over You" started up. To John's bewilderment, Grover pulled her close, even resting his head on her head.

When Wayne excused himself to go to the men's room, Virgie and Martha went to the dance floor, leaving John and Cindy at the table.

"Don't worry, you don't have to ask me to dance," Cindy said. "My feet are sore."

"Are you sure?" John asked. "I'm probably good for one more."

"I'm on my feet all the time."

"You're not retired?"

"I wish," she said with a groan. "I'm a registered nurse over at Riverside Methodist. I plan to work until I'm seventy, if I can make it that far."

"You must love your work." He noticed a small caduceus tattoo inside her right wrist.

"Let's not get carried away," she said. "But yes, I do love being a nurse, but it gets more difficult the older I get. Do you have any idea what it's like turning over a three-hundred-pound person in bed?"

"I can't say I do, or that I'd want to."

"My husband died from pancreatic cancer almost four years ago," she said. "We had good insurance, but it still drained a lot of our savings. I also have a daughter who recently moved back in with me with two kids after going through a nasty divorce. Those are the reasons I still put on scrubs five days a week."

"I certainly hope things work out for you."

"I wish I had known you and Virgie better in high school. You guys are so much fun."

"We were a couple goofballs back then," John said. "We still are, in some respects."

"I went out with Grover a few times," she said, turning her head toward Sally and Grover. "He was a beast."

"Oh."

"He raped me," she blurted. "I was lucky to get him off me and run away. He acts now like he doesn't know me."

"Maybe you should be glad about that."

"I never thought of it that way," she said. "Just the sight of him makes my skin crawl."

"You didn't call the police or anyone after it happened?"

"I didn't think anyone would believe me." A tear trickled down her cheek. "I was ashamed. I was scared. I didn't know what to do, so I didn't do anything."

"You didn't tell your parents?"

"My mother told me to keep it to myself and said I shouldn't have put myself in that position for it to happen."

"And your father?"

"I never said anything about it to him. Mother told me not to because he would have disowned me."

The song ended and Sally hurried back to the table, Grover a couple steps behind. Cindy turned her head away from him.

"Here she is," Grover said as Sally sat next to John. "I was tempted to take her home with me."

"Thanks for bringing her back in one piece."

"Maybe you can save me another dance for later," Grover said to Sally.

Sally exhaled lightly and turned her head in another direction. "We'll see."

Grover headed over toward the bar while Martha and Virgie returned to their seats.

"I'm ready to go back to the room," Sally said.

"Are you sure?" John asked before realizing he only had to read her face to know she was serious and seething about something.

Sally scurried toward the exit before John waved at the others. "See ya'll tomorrow."

"Hey, don't rush off," Wayne said as those at the table seemed perplexed by Sally and John's sudden departure.

Sally headed directly to the room as John could hardly keep pace. She was already sitting on the edge of the bed when he stepped inside and closed the door.

"Your classmate is a monster," she exclaimed. "Didn't you see him out there?"

"I'm sorry, but I was chatting with Cindy."

"He was trying to feel me up. I think I'm going to take a shower."

"Cindy called him a beast."

"Oh, really?"

"We can talk about it later," John said.

"Your friend practically spoiled the entire weekend for me."

"He's not my friend. He was a bully in high school."

"Pardon my language, but he's an asshole now." She began weeping. "I've never been treated like that."

John sat and placed an arm around her. "It's going to be okay. I'll say something to him tomorrow."

"No, please don't," she said, wiping away tears with her fingers. "We're going to get through this weekend."

"We can leave tomorrow morning if you want to," he said. "You know it wouldn't bother me."

"We're not going to do that, either. We're not going to let him spoil the reunion."

John walked to the bathroom and returned with several tissues. She dabbed the tears from her face and blew her nose.

He comforted her with a gentle squeeze and a kiss on the cheek.

"I'm going to take a shower," Sally said. "I feel dirty all over."

"Is there anything I can do in the meantime?" John said. "Like go back and punch him in the nose?"

"You're being silly now. Let's get through the weekend. Everything'll be fine."

While Sally was taking a shower, John got undressed, turned on the television, and crawled into bed. The more he thought about the situation, the more he could feel his blood pressure rising. He tightened his fists several times before taking several deep breaths to relax. He realized about all he could do at that point would be to confront Grover at the picnic. There would be no turning back on that.

"Feel better?" John asked, clicking off the TV when Sally returned to the bedroom.

"A little," she said, putting on her pajama shorts. "I try not to think about it."

"That's a good idea."

"Easier said than done."

"I know."

She got into bed and snuggled next to John, resting her damp head on his shoulder. The overhead light was still on, but John was reluctant to get up and turn it off because of Sally's state of mind, as well as his own. This was a temporary comfort zone.

"Anything I can get you?" he asked. "Maybe a snack or something from the gift shop?"

"I'm not hungry."

"Let me know if you think of something."

"John, please, can't we just lie her for a while in silence?"

"Sure."

But Sally quickly broke her silence. "There's one more thing."

"What is it?"

"Your friend Grover..."

"I've told you he's not my friend."

"Okay, your ex-classmate then, when he was dancing, had an erection."

John raised up on his elbows. "What?"

"You heard me. It was disgusting."

"How did you know?"

Sally was bewildered by his comment, her eyes practically popping out. "What do you think? I felt him against my body."

"I'm sorry," John said, lowering his head back on the pillow. "I wasn't thinking. You caught me by surprise with that."

"Well, your friend, I mean classmate, really caught me by surprise. Argh!"

"I'm sorry." John softly kissed her forehead.

"I think I'm ready to go to sleep. Can you turn out the light?"

John eased out of bed and flicked the switch. When he returned to bed, Sally had turned over on her side. He placed an arm around her waist. They didn't move for several minutes. John was unsure if she had fallen asleep, or like him, had wandered into quiet thought about the evening. It had turned out to be a memorable evening for the wrong reason.

When John awoke at five-thirty, he was facing the opposite direction as their rear ends touched. He rolled out of bed quietly, not wanting to disturb Sally from her seemingly peaceful slumber. He put on the clothes he had worn the previous evening and tip-toed from the room, hoping the restaurant would be open for coffee.

John couldn't believe his eyes when he saw Virgie sitting on a wooden bench outside the restaurant. He was still in his tux, unbuttoned collar, and bowtie sticking out his breast pocket.

"Mornin'," Virgie said in a restrained manner. "The restaurant doesn't open until six. Have a seat." He tapped the bench.

"Didn't you go to bed last night?" John asked. "Or do you usually sleep in your clothes?"

"I got about two hours of shut-eye."

"So you stayed at the dance for a while?"

"I left about an hour after you. It was clearing out about then, so you might say I helped close the joint." He laughed. "Cindy and I decided it was too early to call it a night, so we went to some dive a mile or so from here. We danced a little, drank some more, and then found a Dunkin' and drank coffee and ate donuts and talked until around three or so."

"A long night for you."

"And Cindy as well," Virgie said, covering his mouth and yawning. "I'm too old for this shit. I'm not sure the last time I pulled an all-nighter."

"Same here, old friend. I think Sally and I were in bed by eleven."

"So what are you doing here so early? I think I'd be sleeping in."

"I'm an early bird. I also wanted to get some coffee. I didn't want to disturb Sally by making a cup in the room."

"There's coffee makers in the rooms?"

"Kind of a standard amenity these days."

"I guess I never paid attention. Easy to operate?"

"If I can do it, anyone can."

"How about let's go to my room and brew some instead of waiting here?"

"That works," John said. "I can't stay for too long because Sally doesn't know where I am."

They strolled to Virgie's room on the second floor. John prepared the two cups of coffee while Virgie stood to the side and watched. "That's easy enough," he said. "Learn something new all the time."

They sat near the foggy patio window. Virgie opened the curtains, letting in the sun's soft morning glow peeking through distant pine trees.

"Sally and I had a problem last night," John said after taking a sip from his cup.

"Serious?"

"Grover tried to put some moves on her."

"Where? I thought she was with you all the time."

"On the dance floor."

"I recall them now on the floor," Virgie said. "Martha and I were out there as well. So what happened?"

"He was trying to do more than dance with her. You know, trying to touch her where he shouldn't. She was upset. We left right after it happened."

"We wondered why you guys cut out so fast. So what are you going to do?"

"I think she wants to let it slide. I'm not so sure about that. I'm still pissed about it. And I get more upset the more I think about it."

"I can't say I don't blame you. He was an asshole in school, and he's an asshole now. Assholes never change unless they become bigger assholes."

"I never thought of it that way, but you're right."

"Is he going to be at the picnic this afternoon?" Virgie asked.

"I assume so," John said. "I'll confront him about it if he is. I don't know what else I can do other than to let him know we didn't appreciate it."

"Damn," Virgie said before a sip from his cup. "That really pisses me off the more I think about it. He's such an asshole."

"You've said that," John said, unable to suppress a smile.

"I just needed to say it again."

"That's what Sally called him when we got back to the room, and that's a word she never uses."

"Is there something I can do?"

"I'm not asking you to do anything. You don't need to get involved. I was just letting you know what happened. I needed to get it off my chest. Vent some."

"If you say so."

"Did Cindy tell you anything about Grover?"

"She's never mentioned him." Virgie said.

"Well, there's something else. I probably shouldn't tell you this." Virgie tilted his head. "What?"

"This is between the two of us, but she told me that Grover raped her in high school."

Virgie was silent for a few seconds as if in a trance. "She never talked about that to me."

"That was years ago, but it just shows that some people never change."

Virgie rose from this chair with clenched fists. "I'm really pissed off now."

"I'm sorry, Virgie. I shouldn't have said anything," John said. "Is she going to be at the picnic?"

"I believe so, unless she's too tired. We got to talking and time just slipped away. She has to work later."

"Any intentions of seeing her after the reunion?"

"Are you trying to play matchmaker?" Virgie said with a light laugh.

"I sure sound that way," John said. "I don't mean to. You and she seemed to hit it off really well, especially spending most of the night together."

"That's okay. We were just reminiscing about our time at old Riley High. She filled me on some of the graduates I lost track of."

"You can fill me in later at the picnic, but I need to go back to my room. Sally's probably wondering where I went."

"I need to get out of this tux and get a few hours' sleep before the picnic."

John got up from his chair. "It should be an interesting day."

"It probably will provide a few surprises."

Nineteen

Sally was in her peach-colored pajamas, sitting in a chair by the window. The curtains were pulled back, creating a luminous glow that gave her an ethereal appearance as John came into the room.

"Where have you been?" she asked.

"I didn't want to disturb you when I woke up, so I went to the restaurant," he said. "It wasn't open, but I did see Virgie. We ended up in his room and chatted for a bit. Want me to make you some coffee or would you prefer going to the restaurant for breakfast?"

"How about both?" she said. "I wouldn't mind a cup before getting dressed."

"No problem," he said as he picked up a cup and went to the bathroom sink to fill it with water.

"How's Virgie this morning?" she asked.

"Would you believe he spent the night talking to Cindy?"

"Not really. They seemed to hit it off pretty well."

"That's what I told him. He said they talked about old times and lost track of time."

"That's easy to do."

"She had an encounter with Grover in high school," John blurted.

Sally crinkled her eyes. "Did Virgie tell you?"

"No, she did last night while you were dancing with him. She alleged that he raped her."

"Why do you newspaper folks always use alleged so much? It can be infuriating to people, especially victims."

"Because alleged is one person's side of an event. The other person hasn't been asked, or, if so, denied the accusation. Newspapers and other media can't simply take one person's side unless, in many cases, it's been determined, one way or another, in a court of law. Does that answer your question?"

"But we're two people sitting here, and what we say is simply between the two of us. We're not going to court over anything."

"But what if I didn't say alleged, and you repeated it to someone else?"

"You're incorrigible at times, John Ross. It makes me want to pull out my hair. Always by the book."

"But I just want to set the record straight. I don't want to be spreading false news."

"Ha ha." Sally rolled her eyes. "Please, John, let's move on. You've made your point, and I know what you mean. Perhaps I should say that Grover allegedly groped me on the dance floor. Then you can ask him later for his version of what happened."

John inhaled a deep breath, then quietly prepared her coffee, putting in a packet of creamer and half-packed of sugar. He walked over and handed it to her, then sat on the other chair. They stared at each other for a few seconds with impassive expressions.

"I see your point as well, sweetheart. I'm not doubting you. In fact, I've never disbelieved you about anything. You know that."

"So what else did Cindy say about your, uh, classmate?"

"She didn't go into any detail other than having had to fight him off. She says he totally ignores her now, as if she doesn't exist."

"Maybe I should be so lucky this afternoon."

"I plan to say something to him."

"John, it's not worth it. Let it rest."

"We'll see."

"I should have done something last night, but he caught me by surprise. I was shocked more than anything. Thinking back on it, I should have kneed him between the legs. At the least, I should have pushed him off me and walked away."

"Why didn't you?"

"Huh?"

"Never mind."

"John, like I said, I was in a momentary state of shock. And furthermore, and I know this is lame, I didn't want to cause a scene around your classmates."

"I understand, I think."

"Well, think some more. We don't behave like that and never will."

"To a point."

Sally set her coffee on the table. "I'm getting a little hungry. I'm going to get dressed and we can go to the restaurant."

"While you do that, I'm going to take a quick shower and change into some clean clothes."

Twenty minutes later, John and Sally walked down the hall to the crowded lobby, where people were standing in line to check out or milling about the area. He overhead someone say the Buckeyes had won the game in a nail biter.

Stepping into the restaurant, they were told by the hostess there was a twenty-minute wait to be seated. John glanced over the room and noticed Barrett and Gloria Bozarth waving at them from a booth. As they approached the couple, Barrett said, "As you can see, this place is packed. Why don't you join us?"

"Don't mind if we do," John said, as Sally eased into the bench seat. "We sure appreciate it."

"Did you enjoy the dinner last night?" Gloria asked.

"For the most part," John said. "How about you two?"

"Between us, the dinner was somewhat flavorless, but that's to be expected at these kinds of activities, I suppose," Barrett said. "The dance was okay, if that's what you want to do. We preferred going from table to table and chatting with old friends. Other than that, we had a pleasant time."

"Didn't you leave a little early?" Gloria asked, glancing first at John and then Sally.

"It was getting past our bedtime," John said with a chuckle. "Right, Sally?"

Her eyes stayed on the menu. "Yes, hon."

"So you missed the rowdiness," Barrett said.

"How so?" John said. Sally lowered the menu.

"Grover Jones apparently had too much to drink and threw up on one of the tables. It was nasty."

"I'm glad we missed it."

"Bubba Miller wished he had as well."

"I didn't see Bubba at the dinner."

"He was there with a wife or significant other. They were sitting at the table where Grover vomited and got some of the splatter. Bubba went after him and several guys had to keep them apart, especially after Bubba's significant other splashed her drink all over Grover. He wasn't happy about that."

"Good for her."

"I believe Bubba had been drinking too much as well."

A waitress came to the table with a carafe of coffee and cups for John and Sally and took all their orders. They sat quietly for a couple minutes as if in thought, preparing and sipping their coffees.

"I recall Grover and Bubba being good friends in high school," John said, breaking the silence. "Grover was more of the leader, while Bubba was more of an instigator."

"You mean, more like a weasel," Barrett said with a laugh. "He'd say a lie about someone saying something about Grover and then tell him."

"Is Bubba his real name?" Gloria asked.

"Shirley."

Gloria giggled. "Are you serious?"

"That's it," John said. "Can you understand why he'd prefer Bubba?"

"I think Shirley is fine, but if you're a bully or punk, that's not a good name."

"I believe they came together," Barrett said. "But they sure didn't leave together."

"They had to call security to remove Grover from the room," Gloria said.

"As you can imagine, he wasn't a happy camper," Barrett said.

"Grover must have a serious drinking problem," Gloria said. "He was acting obnoxious before he got sick."

"What was he doing?" John asked.

"Trying to dance with the women and just being loud and despicable. Several people tried to make him be quiet, but then he got vulgar. I'm not going to repeat what he said."

"I'm glad we left when we did."

"I feel sorry for the organizers," Barrett said. "They put in a lot of effort to make this a memorable occasion, and then one person can spoil the whole event for some people."

"I wonder if Grover will be at the picnic?" John asked.

"Your guess is as good as mine. I hope he doesn't attend, but I'm not counting on it."

"What in the world does Bubba do?" John asked.

"Believe it or not, I was told he was in politics on the local level in a small town near here."

"Why doesn't that surprise me?"

"I'm sure he kept things stirred up."

A waiter brought their breakfast orders. They sat quietly and ate for several minutes as the restaurant crowd began to thin.

"Are you going to play softball today?" John asked.

"You can't be serious," Barrett said with a strong laugh. "I played golf yesterday and it drained me. I was never much of a ball player other than golf. Actually, I preferred chess. Did you play any sports?"

"Some baseball, but that was about it."

"So you may play softball today?"

"I doubt it. With this heat wave, that's asking for a heart attack or stroke at our age."

"How about you, Sally? I understand it's going to be co-ed."

"I was never much into sports. At least not like the girls are today. We didn't even have any sports other than golf or tennis when I was in high school. Now the girls play most everything the boys do. Our daughter played basketball and fast-pitch softball."

"We didn't have the opportunities the girls have today," Gloria said, raising her thin brows. "But at least women your age fought to make it happen for them."

"Did it happen for you?" Sally asked.

"I was never particularly good in sports. I partook in drama class activities. I aspired to be an actress."

"Did that happen?"

"Not really. I was in some plays in college. They were bit parts so I learned early on that I didn't have a future in films or plays."

"So the afternoon gathering begins at three at Fairwood Park?" Barrett interjected.

"And it should be over by seven or eight," John said.

"I do hope I'll be able to speak to a few more classmates. I saw Dewey Burgess, Pamela Stone, and Mildred Gross last night, but wasn't able to say much other than a quick 'hi' to them because of Grover's antics."

"Same here," John said, taking a sip of coffee.

"Maybe they'll call off the game so people can spend more time with each other."

"I'm not so sure that'll happen. I overheard some of the guys talking about it last night, especially those on the baseball team. We had some rather good jocks in our school, or they thought they were."

"Speaking of athletes, have you seen Benji Walton?" Barrett asked. "He may have been the best overall athlete in school. I think he even went on to play quarterback at a mid-major college."

"Someone told me that he still lives in the area but has Parkinson's. I'm not sure he'll be able to attend in that condition, or if he'd want to."

"We should find out where he lives and pay him a visit."

"I'll check the class directory when I get back to the room."

"Maybe we can persuade him to come to the picnic," Barrett said.

"It's worth a try."

Twenty

John and Barrett had decided to meet in front of the motel in two hours. Barrett mentioned that Gloria wanted to attend Mass at a downtown church. For John and Sally, it was getting in a morning walk at a small park across the road to work off some of the breakfast calories. It also gave him time to find out where Benji lived.

The morning was already off to a sultry start as they both began perspiring minutes after leaving the motel, despite moving at a leisurely pace. There were several joggers, all sweating profusely in the heavy air, as well as a few walkers meandering along the wide, dirt paths.

"I'm not sure this was a good idea," John said, wiping moisture from his brow. "I'll have to take a shower before going back out with Barrett."

"Did you call him Barrett in high school?" Sally asked.

"He was always Barry back then. I was called Johnny while growing up, but you've always known me as John. Did you have a nickname?"

"A few people would call me Sal, but for the most part, I've been Sally."

"I'm sure I've been called a few choice names behind my back," John said. "And to be honest, to my face."

"You shouldn't think that."

"I remember Sister Cathy's son calling me boomer, as if it would hurt my feelings. I consider it a badge of honor now."

"As it should be. There's nothing wrong with growing older."

"Simply another stage in life."

"Enjoy it while you can."

"And then you die."

"John, you didn't have to say that."

"It's the truth."

"Have you ever considered it an unspoken truth?"

"Oh, well..."

"You won't admit that I'm right."

"I don't know what to say," he said, shrugging.

"Then don't say anything."

"What did you think about the ruckus at the reunion involving Grover?" John asked.

"I suppose that explains his behavior toward me. Like I told you, he smelled of liquor when I danced with him. But that's still no excuse for the way he acted toward me or anyone else. It was disgusting and demeaning."

"I'm going to say something to him about it at the picnic," John said. "And don't try to talk me out of it. I've made up my mind."

"Oh, John, what difference would it make? Why don't we just try to avoid him for a few hours and then be on our merry way? He's not worth the time nor effort. We'll never see him again."

"It's more than that for me. It's a matter of principle and honor. I'd have trouble looking at myself in the mirror if I let it pass. My only regret is that I didn't go back to the dance after you told me. That's been in my craw ever since."

Sally frowned. "I almost wish I hadn't said anything to you until we got home."

"That would have really pissed me off, and you know that."

"Maybe so, but I don't think you would have been able to say or do anything about it."

"Don't be so sure. I do draw the line on what I'll tolerate before I act."

"Just be careful what you say."

"I plan to, but it depends on how Grover responds."

"Maybe we should have gone home this morning."

"Speaking of home, I wonder what's going on there today," John said. "My guess is that Wendell and Libby are at church and your mother is watching some religious service on TV."

"I hope that's what they're doing right now," Sally said. "I'll give Mother a call when you're out with Barrett."

"I hope all is normal, or at least normal for our family."

"As you like to say, no news is good news."

"You're getting more like your mother by the day," John said, gently elbowing her.

"It keeps you on your toes, wise guy."

They stopped and sat on a cast-iron bench shadowed by a large maple tree. A young man with a Labrador retriever on a leash marched toward them, as the walker tugged on the restraint to keep the canine from invading their area. John reached out and patted the dog's head several times before they moved on down the path at a vigorous pace.

"That makes me wonder if anyone has taken the time to take Whiskers out while we've been away," John said.

"I wouldn't count on it, although Mother is good about letting him out every few hours so he can go potty."

"What would you think about checking out of the motel tonight and driving back home? There probably won't be as much traffic."

"Let me think about it, but my initial response is to spend the night. We're likely to be tired after the picnic, and I don't like the idea of driving in the dark for three or four hours."

"I'll be doing the driving," John said.

"Like I said, I don't like the idea of driving in the dark."

"There you go again. Being a smart aleck."

"You know I'm right."

"You think?" he said, his brows furrowed.

"There's no hurry to get back home. We can get up early in the morning and leave, maybe stop along the way for breakfast."

"Well, give it some more thought and let me know if you change your mind."

"I will," she said, "but don't count on it."

"I never do."

"Now who's being the smart aleck!"

"Got room for two more there?" came a breathless voice from twenty feet away. Wayne and Martha moseyed toward them, slightly hunkered, seeking respite from the heat.

John and Sally scooted over, making for a tight squeeze.

"We thought this would be a good idea, just to kill some time before going to the picnic," Martha said, fanning her face with her hand. "Now I'm not so sure."

"I know what you mean," John said. "The best of intentions."

"We've all had them throughout our lives," Wayne said.

"Uh-oh," Martha said. "Wayne and John are about to wax philosophic."

"Martha doesn't appreciate my wisdom," Wayne said, tilting his head.

"Sally is the same way," John said.

"I appreciate Wayne's wisdom," Sally said, grinning.

"I meant my wisdom," John said. "Or lack thereof."

"I wish my wisdom included a bottle of water," Wayne said.

"Is it safe to say your wisdom doesn't runneth over?" John asked.

"You are proving my point," Sally said to John. "We didn't bring water, either."

"Are you guys enjoying the reunion?" Martha asked.

"For the most part," John said. "I think the organizers have done an incredible job putting all this together. When things move along smoothly, that generally means they've put in a lot of work."

"The turnout seems to be good," Wayne said. "Someone told me about sixty percent of our class showed up, although about seventy-five percent indicated they would be here."

"That's probably about par for the course," John said.

"We almost didn't come. After fifty years, you lose so many connections with people. But Martha insisted we should attend. And it was time for us to reconnect with valid excuses to give our spouses."

"Our daughter arranged this for us, so we had to come," John said.

"You had mixed feelings as well?" Martha asked.

"I haven't had any connections with them since I left in sixty-eight," John said. "I'm not saying that's a good thing. Like most of them, I moved on to other things, such as family and career. And I didn't think I'd have much in common with anyone because we all have grown and developed different interests."

"That's sorta how I felt," Wayne said with a shrug.

"But then I told Wayne he should have a different attitude," Martha said. "I told him to be curious and see how people changed over the years."

"But my main reason was to be with you," Wayne said, pecking Martha on the cheek.

"Me, too, but I wanted to see others as well. This might be our last opportunity unless someone decides to hold another reunion. You never know what can happen to prevent it from happening."

"A hundred years ago, there was a flu pandemic that killed millions of people," Sally said. "It was called the Spanish flu."

"I'm not concerned about something like that happening," Wayne said. "That was then, this is the twenty-first century. Highly unlikely. Medicine and healthcare have advanced a lot since then."

"I hope you're right," John said. "But life can be unpredictable."

"You're waxing philosophic again," Martha said, grinning.

"You got me on that."

"Just having fun."

"I know," he said with a nod. "Old folks like to share their sage lessons from life."

"You know, some people take things way too seriously," Martha said. "That's what I explained to Wayne. It's interesting to come across people from one's past, no matter at what point you first knew them, and see how they've changed. It's almost like reading a book and getting to final chapters."

"You're right," John said. "I've reconnected with some old friends I hope to stay connected to. And, to be honest, a few I hope never to see again."

They all laughed.

"You must have heard about the dance last night," Wayne said. "It was either a night to remember, or one to forget."

"We left before things got too unruly," John said. Sally gazed off into the distance.

"You should have stayed," Martha said. "We sat at the corner table and observed what was going on. I didn't remember some of the people, so Wayne gave me a running account as everything happened. It was entertaining, to say the least."

"We heard about Grover," John said, glancing at Sally.

"Things settled down after he was escorted from the premises," Wayne said. "But there were a few classmates who came separately and left with someone else. Remember Sarah Ponder?"

"Vaguely," John said. "Wasn't she a cheerleader?"

"She's been married a few times over the years," Wayne said. "She got a little wild on the dance floor. Apparently, she had too much to drink because she was putting on some, er, sexy moves with a few dance partners."

"I'd say their wives didn't appreciate it," Martha said.

"Maybe we left too soon," John said, wriggling his brows.

"I don't think so," Sally replied, giving him a disbelieving glance. "You're right."

"And I didn't know Cecil Menifee was gay," Wayne said.

"That's news to me," John said. "Although I haven't seen or heard from him since we graduated."

"That man with him was his spouse," Martha said. "They've been married for several years."

"How did you find that out?"

"They came over and sat with us and while discussing what was happening in our lives, Cecil casually mentioned that Christian, his partner, was also his spouse," Martha said. "They live in Minneapolis."

"I would have never guessed that," John said. "But again, I'm generally oblivious to those things."

"They seem happy," Wayne said.

John glanced at his watch. "We hate to leave good company, but I've got someplace to go in about an hour and I need to get cleaned up."

John and Sally rose from the bench, but were forced a couple feet to the side to avoid being struck by three young bicyclists racing down the path.

"I should alert you that Tyrone was in the front lobby when we left, recruiting classmates and others for a church service he was going to conduct in one of the conference rooms," Wayne said.

"Thanks for the heads-up. We'll try to enter through a side entrance."

As soon as they walked into their motel room, off came their clothes. John adjusted the shower temperature and stepped back to let Sally go in first. They both turned around several times under the lukewarm spray to rinse off the sweaty oils from their bodies.

"This is going to be a long day if it doesn't cool off," Sally said. "I may have to let you go to the picnic by yourself."

"Uh, nice try, sweetheart, but I don't think so," John said. "We're in this together now."

"You can't blame a girl for trying."

"You'll be able to rest in air-conditioned comfort while I'm out with Barrett. Maybe we'll get some rain between now and the picnic."

"Maybe you should go to Tyrone's church service and pray for rain."

John dropped his head in amusement. "You bet!"

After the shower, Sally opted to only put on her underwear and got under the sheets. John donned a pair of khakis and a pastel yellow polo shirt and headed to the front entrance to the hotel to meet Barrett.

Tyrone had adjourned his makeshift church minutes earlier and was standing outside the conference room shaking hands with congregants, most of whom John didn't recognize. Apparently, Tyrone, with assistance from Sister Maggie, had done a good job recruiting motel guests to his hour of prayer.

"We missed you at our service, John," Tyrone said. "We got a blessed start to our day."

"I didn't realize you were going to have a service."

"I announced it last night after that dreadful, and might I add sinful, altercation at the dinner. Maggie and I believed it would help to deliver an uplifting message from the good Lord's book."

"Sally and I didn't hear about it until this morning. We left the dinner early."

"I must say you and your wife were fortunate not to witness what happened. It was disgusting, and a disgrace to Riley High School graduates."

"I guess you might say we were blessed in a different way," John said. Tyrone eyed him thoughtfully, but didn't say anything.

Barrett pulled his vehicle out front, parked, and stepped inside the entrance. He waved at John. "Ready?"

"I need to go," John said to Tyrone. "I'll see you later at the picnic."

John followed Barrett through the entrance and got into a black Cadillac Escalade SUV Barrett had rented for his visit. John handed him Benji's address, which Wayne punched into the vehicle's GPS.

"Have you given any thought to investment opportunities for retirement we discussed earlier?" Barrett asked along the way.

"I've been focused on the reunion and seeing old friends," John said, surprised by the question.

"Don't let the opportunity slip away."

"Thanks. I'll try not to."

Benji resided in the south side suburb of Lincoln Village, about twenty minutes from the motel. They located his home in the middle of a row of neat condominiums. Colorful chrysanthemums, asters, and pansies filled box planters attached to bay windows.

"So far so good," Barrett said as he parked in a visitor's space. "I hope he's home."

They walked up a long sidewalk to the front door, and Barrett rang the doorbell two times. John noticed a small sign in the window that read "No Solicitors" and pointed it out to Barrett. Barrett shrugged and pushed the button again.

"Can't you read the sign?" a loud but wavering voice came from inside the door. "I don't want any."

"We're not selling anything," Barrett said.

"I don't want any religion either."

"Amen, brother," John said. "We don't either."

The door creaked open three inches, held in place by a chain lock. They could see a man's eye peek at them.

"Benji Walton?" Barrett asked.

"I haven't been called that for years. It's Ben Walton now."

"Well, do you remember Barry Bozarth and Johnny Ross?"

There was a click and the door swung open. Ben stood in the doorway with a wide grin, clutching a cane. "Oh, my goodness. What in the world are you guys doing here?"

"First of all, we're dropping in unannounced to visit you," John said. "I hope that's okay with you."

"Well, sure, guys." Ben unlocked the screen door and pushed it open until John grabbed the latch. Ben backed away as John held the door open for Barrett and followed him inside the home. Ben's shaky hand pointed them to the living room to the left of the foyer.

"Nice place you have," Barrett said, as he sat on one end of the couch and glanced around at the surroundings. John sat at the other while Ben shuffled over to a large, chocolate-colored recliner. Ben was thinner than his high school days, and his thick black hair had more than a fair share of white strands. He wore a bushy moustache that needed trimming as it nearly covered his upper lip.

"I like it here," Ben said. "It's a safe neighborhood, for the most part. As you can probably tell, I don't get out much other than to the doctor."

"We're in town for our fiftieth class reunion and wondered why you weren't there," John said. "Folks have been asking about you."

"Class reunion?" Ben said with a perplexed expression. "That's news to me."

"Invitations went out last year," Barrett said. "You didn't receive one?"

"Like I said, this is the first I've heard about it. I have a housekeeper who goes through my mail. I don't think she would throw it away, but you never know."

"There's going to be picnic and softball game today at Fairwood Park. Why don't you go with us?"

"I'm not much of a softball player," Ben said with a short laugh. "As you can probably tell."

"We're not sure if we're going to play," John said. "But wouldn't it be great time to see some of your old classmates?"

"I don't know." Ben glanced at his trembling hands.

"Oh, come on, it'll be a nice time. Everyone would love to see you. Don't forget, you were the star athlete in our class."

"That was many moons ago. I ain't what I used to be." Ben lowered his head.

"Who is?" Barrett said, tapping his belly.

"Am I dressed okay?" Ben said. He was wearing baggy cream-colored shorts, white crew socks pulled over his calves, and a faded Cleveland Indians T-shirt.

"You look fine to me," John said. "I'm sure most of the folks will be wearing leisure clothes."

"Okay, then, but let me go to the bathroom and brush my teeth and comb my hair." Ben rose slowly from the chair and wobbled his way out of the living room and down the hallway.

The living room was a neat and orderly room consisting of couch, recliner, a flat screen TV attached to the wall, and a fireplace with an electric insert. On the mantel was a row of framed photographs, including one of Ben in a quarterback pose, his arm cocked back holding a football, probably from a newspaper or publicity shot from his college days.

Ben returned after twenty minutes. Besides time in the bathroom, he had changed his clothes to jeans, a long-sleeved Oxford blue shirt, and a Columbus Clippers baseball cap.

"You sure look sporty," Barrett said.

Benji laughed. "I couldn't leave looking like I did. People would think I was homeless."

"Who cares what they think?"

"I do."

"I understand what you mean," John said. "How we dress at home and in public can differ a lot."

"Would you mind rolling up the sleeves for me?" Ben asked. "It's kinda hard to do in my condition."

Barrett rolled up each sleeve just below the elbows as Ben stood as motionless as he could. "It's going to be a warm day, so that's probably a good idea," Barrett said when finished and stepped back.

Barrett walked ahead of John and Ben as they headed to the car. He opened the passenger door for Ben and helped him into the vehicle.

"Nice car you drive," Ben said, as Barrett helped fasten the seatbelts.

"It's a rental."

"What's your other car?"

"I drive a mid-sized Mercedes."

"Impressive."

"It's just a car."

"If you say so," Ben said with a chuckle as Barrett drove the SUV out of the parking lot. "My last car was a Chevy Cavalier."

"What have you been up to all these years?" John asked, leaning forward in the backseat behind Ben.

"I tore my knee up during my senior year of college. That ruined my chances for the pros, even though I was a longshot. I thought I might have a chance for the Canadian Football League. But that went kaput."

"Sorry to hear that," Barrett said. "I knew you were doing well at Akron, and then I lost track of you. So that's what happened."

"It really messed up my plans. I got so depressed I didn't even finish college."

"So what did you do?" John asked.

"I became a trucker, you know, driving those big semis all across the country. I did that for nearly thirty years. It was a helluva job until it started messing with my kidneys."

"Marry?"

"Yeah, I got hitched with some gal in Nebraska. She ran a truck stop outside of Lincoln. That's where I met her. We stayed together until 2009. That's when I started showing symptoms of this damn Parkinson's. I couldn't drive anymore after a few years, so we came back here."

"Where is she now?" Barrett asked.

"After we divorced, she moved back to Nebraska. She said she was homesick, but I think she got tired of taking care of me. She wasn't much help because she drank all the time and watched TV. I was glad to see her leave."

"Any children?" John asked.

"We have a son and daughter. The boy lives in Westerville and the girl's in Youngstown. I don't see much of them. My daughter-in-law drops in every few weeks to check on me, but that's about it."

Barrett pulled the Cadillac into a temporary guest parking space in front of the motel. John assisted Ben in getting out of the truck and accompanied him to the front lobby. It was about one-thirty, so they still had nearly an hour and a half before the reunion activities at Fairwood Park.

As they walked toward one of the benches to sit and wait for Barrett to park and show up in the lobby, Tyrone rushed over from the side and lifted a startled Ben off his feet before John could caution him.

"If it ain't Benji Walton," Tyrone said with a broad smile. "What a blessing to see you again, brother."

Ben, his head slightly bobbing, said in a trembling voice, "It's great to see you, Ty. It's been a lot of years. You look damn good."

Tyrone's eyes began to well, and he bit his lower lip as he studied his old friend. "You look good too, brother."

Barrett showed up and said he needed to go to his room and check on Martha. "I shouldn't be gone too long," he said. "Don't leave without me."

"Don't forget me," Ben said with a laugh.

"If you'll excuse me as well, I need to check in on my wife," John said. "I think you're in good hands."

Sally was lying in bed dressed in knee-high shorts and a tank top, reading *Cosmopolitan*. The TV, turned to a political program, was on mute. That was fine by John, who was getting tired of the rancor from the left and right sweeping the country. He sat on a chair and propped his feet on the other.

"Did you see your old friend?" Sally asked, setting the magazine to her side.

"He came back with us. He's in the lobby. Did I tell you he has Parkinson's?"

"You may have mentioned it."

"He's a bit slow getting around, but that's to be expected. He lives alone, so that's kinda sad."

"I can't wait to meet him."

After going to the bathroom, John and Sally ventured back out of the room and to the lobby, where several more classmates staying at the motel had congregated, mostly around Ben. They were all casually dressed in one way or another, depending on their perceived social and financial status, ranging from preppy to redneck but most in between.

Ben sat on bench near the gift shop, appearing somewhat dazed by all the attention as he chatted and shook hands with former classmates. Several took out smartphones and snapped photos with him. He noticed John and motioned with his hand for him to come over.

"I'd like for you to meet my wife, Sally," John said. Sally smiled, reached out and shook Ben's hand.

"It's my pleasure," Benji said, smiling.

"How's everything going?"

Ben motioned for John to bend down.

"Can you take me to the men's room," he whispered in John's ear.

"Not a problem," John said. "I can even take you down to my room."

"That's too far. I don't think I could make it, if you know what I mean."

John held Ben's hand and guided him to the men's room. Ben went to a stall and closed the door.

"Let me know if you need any assistance," John said.

"I can handle it from here," Ben said. "But thanks for asking. Not many folks do that."

After a couple minutes, and feeling like he was intruding on Ben's privacy, John stepped out of the restroom.

"Everything okay?" Sally asked.

"Nature calling. I'll check on him in a few minutes."

Barrett and Gloria showed up in the lobby, dashing in the latest designer outfits, Barrett in white Ralph Lauren slacks and soft pink Tommy Hilfiger polo shirt while Gloria wore navy Calvin Klein ankle pants and white Alexander Wang T-shirt. John knew they wouldn't be playing softball or doing much else other than handing out business cards.

"Where's Benji?" Barrett asked.

"Restroom," John said.

"Do you mind if he rides with you to the picnic?"

"That's not a problem."

"I promised the organizers to pick up a couple cases of pop and tea, so I need to go now. We'll see you there."

As they walked away, John returned to the men's room, where Ben was still in the stall. John noticed his pants were drooped around his ankles.

"Everything okay?" John asked.

"No."

"What's the matter?"

"I can't get up," Ben said. "Can you help me?"

"Sure."

John heard Ben unlatch the door and pushed it open. Ben sat with troubled eyes.

"This is embarrassing," Ben said. "I should have stayed at home."

"It's not a big deal," John said as he grabbed hold of Ben's underwear and pants and pulled them up around his knees. Ben placed his arms around John's shoulders and lifted up.

The restroom door opened and a man walked toward the stalls, apparently oblivious to John and Ben a few yards away. He stopped abruptly, eyes wide by the unexpected scene.

"What the…" he bellowed, storming out of the room.

"It's not what it appears," John shouted to deaf ears.

"I don't think he heard you," Ben said, letting out a hearty chuckle.

"Oh well, such is life."

"Screw him if he can't take a joke," Ben said.

"You've got that right, old pal."

"The problem is that these toilets sit too low. The one at home sits high. That's why I couldn't get up."

"Don't worry about it," John said, stepping back. Ben zipped up his pants, fastened his belt buckle and walked over to the sink.

"I'm still not sure this was a good idea," Ben said with a fretful expression.

"What?"

"Going to this reunion picnic. I'm getting tired already."

"Would you like to go back to my room and rest for a bit? I don't want you to overdo it."

"I think that would be nice," Ben said with a weary expression. "One more thing, Johnny."

"What's that?"

"Would you take me back home if it gets to be too much?"

"Certainly," John said. "Just let me know."

As they left the restroom, several other classmates came over to see Ben. John walked over and told Sally of their plans and returned a minute later.

"Hey folks, I need to take Benji back to my room for a bit," John said. "We'll see you at the park in a little while."

"We'll see," said Roland, who seemed put off by the remark and walked away.

"Ben seems upset," Sally whispered in John's ear.

"He needs to take a break. Too much excitement going on."

"How about if I ask Virgie to give me a ride to the park? Then you can take your time."

"Where is he?"

"I spoke with him while you were with Ben. He offered to take me if something came up."

"Good deal," John said. "I'll see you in an hour or so, or whenever we get there."

After John and Ben got to the room, John cleared off the unused bed. Ben sat on the edge, then rolled over with his head on a pillow. He exhaled slowly as a relaxed smile crossed his face.

"Thanks for doing this," Ben said, as John removed his friend's brown penny loafers.

"I need a break, too. I'm glad these things only come along every fifty years."

"So this is your first one?"

"Afraid so. You've been to others?

"I went to our tenth and fifteenth," Ben said. "Not many people showed up, especially the ones I wanted to see. It was depressing, too, because a few of them had already passed away."

"I was too busy with other things to return. I know it sounds selfish because there were a few friends I would have like to have seen back then. Oh well, that's water under the bridge. Nothing I can do about it now."

"Do you know if Judy Ratterman showed up?"

"Yeah. I saw her when I checked in. A few others saw her, too. I have to say she's not friendly."

"Oh, that doesn't surprise me," Ben said. "But I would like to see her again. We dated back in the day."

"I didn't know that. I learn something new every day." He chuckled.

"It was secretive. We'd meet at the movie theater, maybe a park."

"I never found much time to date, so you did more than me."

"How does she look?"

"She's rather attractive. Are you still interested in her?"

"Hey, Johnny, that was a long time ago when I was the star athlete. I'm not what I used to be, and I don't think she'd be interested in me now. You know what I'm saying?"

"I hear ya, but you never know. I guess you'll find out later."

"Maybe."

Twenty-one

"I was surprised Judy left early in our senior year." John said.

"Me, too," Ben said. "She had broken up with me by then. I heard her father got transferred to another city. She never wrote or anything, so I lost touch with her. I guess she didn't want to see or hear from me again."

"We were so young that maybe she got another boyfriend after she departed and decided to end things with you all together."

"Man, you can be so harsh," Ben said, shaking his head.

"That's what Sally says. She blames that on me being in the news business, just seeing things as they are and not sugar-coating. I tend to be blunt about things. I didn't mean to hurt your feelings."

"Nah. And you're probably right. She probably dumped me. We all move on to other things. I know I did, so that's probably what she did, too. Like you said, we were just kids. We had lots of growing up to do."

"I sure know I did. Sally would say I still do."

"Mind if I close my eyes for about twenty minutes?" Ben mumbled.

"Go ahead," John said. "I'll step out of the room for a few minutes, then we can go to the picnic if you're up to it."

John closed the curtain and left the room, glancing at his watch to check the time, and strolled to the lobby. He sat on a bench near the rear, in front of a manmade waterfall and floral display.

"Ain't you going to the picnic?" Lenny asked, approaching him from the side wearing frayed cutoff jeans, a multi-colored Rock and Roll Hall of Fame T-shirt, and scuffed leather sandals.

"I'll be heading there in about twenty minutes or so," John said. "Waiting on a friend. How about you?"

"I'm not sure," Lenny said, scratching the side of his head. "My truck won't start. Dead battery, I think."

"If you can't get it started, you're welcome to go with me. Do you want me to see if we can jump it?"

"Sure, that's cool, dude."

John followed Lenny to his truck at the far end of the parking lot. The old Chevy was multi-rusted, with pieces of gray duct tape covering several gaps as well as holding up the driver's side rearview mirror. Lenny popped open the hood, revealing an engine coated in deep oil-covered grime and a battery that had an expiration date of 2015.

"I'm not hopeful," John said. "Do you have jumper cables?"

"None of those, dude," Lenny said. "I was hoping you did."

"I think I do unless someone removed them from the trunk," John said. "Let me go get my SUV."

John walked back to his car, opened the rear entry, and pulled out the cables. He drove back to Lenny's truck, parked in front, and opened his hood. They connected the cables to the batteries in each vehicle but could barely get Lenny's motor to turn over.

"Last time I had to keep it connected for about five minutes," Lenny said, with a hopeful expression.

"We can do that," John said. "But I believe you probably need to get a new battery. This one appears shot."

"You're probably right," Lenny said, shaking his head. "How much does a new battery cost."

"Depends on where you buy one. The average is probably a hundred and fifty dollars."

"That much? Wow!" Lenny said, shaking his head in disbelief. "I think I paid about eighty for this one."

"They're a bit more expensive now."

"No shit."

Lenny got back in this truck, and after turning the ignition four or five times, the engine came to life after a few burps and a trail of black smoke shooting out the tailpipe. He raised his brows in a bright grin and gave a thumbs up on both hands.

John disconnected the cables, closed both of the hoods, and walked around to Lenny behind the wheel. He glanced inside at the floorboard and passenger seat littered with paper cups, wrappers, and crumpled fast-food bags.

"We got her running," Lenny said.

"Mind if I ask you something?"

"What is it?"

"I don't want you to take offense."

"You think I need to run it through a car wash before going to the picnic?"

"No," John said, knowing the truck would probably rip apart under water pressure. "Are you short on cash?"

"I got plenty," Lenny said.

"Enough to replace your battery?"

"Don't have that much."

"There's one of those discount auto parts stores down the road. How about if we run over there now and buy a new one? I don't believe there's much life left in the one you have now."

"I dunno," Lenny said, his mouth twisting.

"I've got you covered."

"Okay, then," Lenny relented with a half smile. "I'll meet you there."

"It's on the right, less than a mile down the road, if memory serves me from the other day."

When John arrived at the parts store several minutes after Lenny, an employee was carrying a battery to install in the truck. John told Lenny to go on to the picnic while he went inside to pay for the battery.

Lenny opened his wallet, pulled out twenty-two dollars and held it out for John.

"You might need it," John said, refusing the cash. "We'll settle it some other time. I'll see you at the picnic."

As Lenny drove off, John followed the employee back into the store.

"That truck is a real piece of crap," the young man said. "That battery is worth more."

"You drive what you can afford," John said, smiling, handing him a credit card. "Be thankful for what you have."

John returned to the motel, finding Ben sitting on the side of the bed and taking a pill with a glass of water.

"How're feeling?" John asked. "Sorry I was gone for so long."

"I thought you left without me," Ben said with a wink.

"I had to give Lenny's truck a jump. Remember Lenny?"

"Yeah, Lenny Lowenstein was a good guy. I think he had some drug problems after coming back from Vietnam. He bounced from job to job. He worked for the sanitation department. I'd see him jumping off and on the back of those big white trucks. It'll be nice seeing him again."

"So you're up and ready to go?"

"I just took my pills to steady my body. Give me a few more minutes."

"Let me know, and then we'll roll."

John went to the bathroom and washed the grunge off his hands, then took a leak, and washed his hands again.

Ben was standing next to the bed when he came back out. "I'm ready," he said. "Let's get this show on the road."

As they drove to Fairwood Park, a light shower started, creating a steamy haze on the roadway. John noticed the picnic shelter in the distance as he pulled into the crowded parking lot.

"We have a bit of a walk ahead of us," John said. "Are you up for it?"

"I can handle it," Ben said.

John removed a small umbrella from the glove compartment and went around to the passenger side to assist Ben. The rain began to pick up as they walked slowly along a narrow graveled path toward the shelter. Classmates were bunched together under the building, most standing and a few sitting on the picnic table benches. Two tables pushed together were reserved for the food and drinks, that were wrapped in containers but conveniently arranged. Four men stood just outside the rear of the shelter holding umbrellas, grilling hamburgers and hot dogs.

Several old friends greeted Ben as he stepped up on the concrete slab and sat at the nearest table. John scanned the crowd until he saw Sally with several women in the far corner. He stepped outside the shelter, opening the umbrella again, and hurried to her side.

"We're calling ourselves the outcasts," Sally said as three women turned to face John.

"Outcasts? Why?"

"Because we're spouses instead of classmates," she said. "We hardly know anyone, so we've banded together to entertain ourselves while the classmates reunite. It works out well for all of us."

"I guess it does," John said. "But I do want you to meet several friends, if you get a chance."

Virgie came over, holding a small bottle of red wine in one hand and a can of Stella Artois in the other, handing it to John. "Thirsty?"

"Thanks," John said, taking the beer. "I assume the softball game has been rained out."

"There are a few guys holding out hope the rain will pass over, but I don't think it will. It seems to be coming down harder."

"You're right," John said. "Where's Cindy?"

Virgie frowned. "I'm not sure if she's going to make it. I talked to her around noon and woke her up. Since she has to go in for the night shift, she may be a no show."

"That's a shame. I was hoping to see her again before Sally and I head back to Lexington."

"Are you leaving after the picnic?"

"I mentioned it to Sally, but I doubt if we will. She doesn't trust my night driving."

"Then that's a good reason to stay tonight."

"Is Judy Ratterman here?"

"She's around here somewhere. She had another gal with her. Why do you want to see her?"

"It's not me. Ben was asking about her."

"Ben?"

"He said they dated some in high school?"

"Really? I never knew that."

"He said it was secretive, so I'm not sure if anyone knows. That's our secret."

"Don't worry." Virgie ran a finger over his mouth like closing a zipper. "It's no one's business, even if it was more than fifty years ago."

John took a swallow of beer. He glanced around the shelter and noticed Grover holding court at a middle table. Two tables over were Wayne and Martha, chatting with Biff and Roland and their spouses. He searched for Lenny and his white ponytail, but he was nowhere to be seen.

"What in the world are they going to do other than eat, since there probably won't be any softball," John asked.

Penny peeked around from behind said, "Maybe we could play spin the bottle."

John turned and grinned. "Now wouldn't that be sight, a bunch of old folks sitting in circles spinning bottles."

"That'd be a hoot," Virgie said.

"Maybe we could substitute hugs for kisses," Penny said with a wide grin and wink.

"Why would we have to spin the bottle to do that?" Virgie said. "Are you wanting a hug?"

"It depends on who's giving the hug," she said, glancing at John before walking away.

"Is she an old flame?" Virgie asked with a snicker.

"She claims I kissed her back in high school," John said. "I don't remember."

Barrett drifted over while Gloria helped the organizers prepare the food tables.

"This thing has bombed," he said, grim-faced. "And it's too damned crowded with folks crammed like sardines. They should have found a larger venue."

"It looks that way," Virgie said.

"Things might pick up if the rain ends," John said. "We really need to circulate and talk to folks before it's over. I wouldn't count on there being other reunions. And if there are, there's no assurances everyone will be there."

"That's rather grim, John," Barrett said. "We're all going to be dead?"

"I didn't say that. It's just that some may be incapacitated for various reasons. Others may choose not to come back. You never know what could happen between now and then."

"Will you?" Virgie asked John.

"I don't like to look too far out in the future."

"I take that as a no," Barrett said.

"I wouldn't go that far. It's just that I don't make commitments I may not be able to keep."

"Fair enough."

The rain dwindled to a light drizzle over the next few minutes, then completely stopped as the overcast clouds opened to splashes of bright sunshine. John glanced out and saw Cindy walking up the path to the shelter.

"It appears you've got a surprise, Virgie," John said, motioning his head in her direction.

Virgie's face glowed as he stepped away from his friends and turned in her direction. "Excuse me, guys."

Twenty-two

"I hope you guys don't mind, but I need to sit," Barrett said as he maneuvered toward a table and past several classmates. "I'm not one to be on my feet all day."

"That's okay by me," John said. "I'm not going anywhere."

A few minutes later, Lenny came bobbing across the damp grass, throwing up his hand to any and all that spotted him. His hair was wet and stringy from the rain.

"What took you so long?" John asked as Lenny stood in front of him with a toothy grin. "I thought you would have gotten here way before me."

"The rain sorta messed things up," he said. "My wipers quit working, so I had to pull off and wait for it to stop."

"You should have called one of us."

"I don't have any of your numbers," Lenny said. "And if I did, the battery on my phone was dead, too. This hasn't been my day except for getting a new battery for my truck."

"How did that happen?" Barrett asked. "Did the battery fairy visit you?'

"You could say that, although I've never considered John a fairy." He let out a light grunt.

"So you're buying batteries for friends today?" Barrett asked John.

"If they need one."

Barrett smirked. "I think I can afford one."

"I can on most days," Lenny said.

"I'd hope I could on any day."

Barrett's snide comments caught John by surprise. "I think we all need a little help now and then. Huh?"

"That's what the Beatles sang about," Lenny said with a laugh. "You remember, a little help from our friends, or something like that."

"Maybe you can get the wipers replaced tomorrow," John said.

"I hope it doesn't rain anymore today so I can make it to the junkyard tomorrow."

"Got enough money to cover it?"

"I'm good," Lenny said. "The son of an old friend runs the place and he lets me get whatever parts I need. I do some odds and ends for him on the weekends."

"That's a good deal," John said.

"And don't worry about the battery, I'll pay you back one way or another. Just give me your address."

"You don't have to pay me back, Lenny. I want you to pay it forward."

"Are you sure?"

"I'm sure."

"So where did you get that beer? I can use a cold one now."

"Back there," John said, rising and pointing in the direction of the food and drinks. "There's several coolers."

"Need one while I'm there?"

"I'm good for right now."

After Lenny left to fetch a beer, Wayne came and sat next to John. "I guess there won't be any softball today, but three of the local guys brought cornhole boards. They're going to be setting those up in a few minutes."

"I never understood how they came up with that name," John said. "I remember my son bringing it up a few years ago, saying he was going to a friend's house to play cornhole. Needless to say, I had to ask him what he was talking about."

"It doesn't have the connotation most people associate with it, especially our generation and older. Did you tell your son?"

"I let it slide. Maybe people will forget what it used to mean."

The three sets of cornhole boards were set parallel from the shelter, the first about twenty feet away.

"Who's up for a cornhole tournament?" Grover shouted, holding three bags up in one hand. Two men had already started playing on the boards farthest away as several others stepped out from under the shelter.

"I'd prefer bridge," a woman said. "Did anyone bring playing cards?"

"Who brings cards to a picnic?" Grover asked.

"He's got a point," Wayne said with a laugh.

"Let's play spin the bottle," a woman hollered from the rear. John figured that suggestion came from Penny, the kissing gal.

"Let's not," Barrett responded amid some laughter.

Virgie and Cindy walked over to John holding soft drinks and sat next to him, catching Grover's attention.

"Hey, Virgie, I bet you're good at cornhole," Grover said, with a booming cackle followed by assorted uneasy snickers from the group.

"What's that supposed to mean?" Virgie asked, tilting his head.

"Don't mind him, Virgie," Cindy muttered. "He's not worth it."

"Did you hear me, Virgie?" Grover asked. "Do you want to play me?"

"I don't know. I heard a long time ago that you were incredibly good at it. In fact, some guys said you couldn't get enough of it."

Grover tossed down the bags and stomped toward Virgie, halting at the edge of the shelter. "What did you say, curly tops?"

"I didn't stutter."

Grover made two long steps into the shelter, standing about ten feet from Virgie. John and Wayne eased closer to Virgie, one on each side.

"You'd better be careful," Grover said, glaring at Virgie.

Virgie shrugged.

The mounting tension broke when Tyrone stood on a table in front of the food, no doubt prompted by the angry words. "May I have your attention, brothers and sisters. We're about to partake of this food."

Several classmates with their backs to him continued talking until they noticed the spreading silence and turned around. Grover, glowering at Virgie, backstepped outside the shelter while John and his friends turned and faced Tyrone, who had been joined by Maggie, holding hands.

"Let's all join hands," Tyrone bellowed, watching over the crowd as people began taking hold of one another's hands. He smiled broadly. "That's better. Now let's bow our heads in prayer."

After a few seconds, when apparently satisfied he had the group's attention, Tyrone began speaking, "Thank you, dear Lord for this great occasion for the nineteen sixty-eight class of Riley High School as it gathers before you for its fiftieth reunion. We remember those who can't be here, be it called to be at your side in heaven or unable to make the journey, for whatever reasons. We ask that you bless the hands of those who prepared this meal. And we pray that when this day is over, you will watch over us as we return to our places of abode. In your holy name, amen."

"Amen," echoed Maggie and a few others in the shelter.

A long line formed on the left side as people picked up paper plates, plastic utensils and napkins and inched toward the food, scooping up coleslaw, deviled eggs, potato salad, watermelon slices, fruit salads, pork and beans, buns, a plate of hotdogs, and stacked hamburgers.

"That's quite a spread," Virgie said.

John watched as Grover and several of his friends hurried to the line. "I hope they save some food for us."

"Good luck with that," Wayne said.

"I'm not sure Gloria and I will eat," Barrett declared.

"Why not?" John asked.

"It's not appetizing to me," he said. "Who knows where all that food was prepared and all those hands have been?"

John grimaced. "Are you trying to take away my appetite?"

"I'll take my chances," Virgie said. "I've made it this far in life. Those folks went to a lot of trouble to set this up. I'll be damned if I'm going to snub my nose at it. Anyway, if anyone gets food poisoning, Cindy will be here to take care of them."

"Let's hope it doesn't come to that," she said. "I have to go to work later on, and I don't want to be sick. But I'm not worried. I'd hope our classmates used good hygiene when preparing their dishes."

"I certainly would hope so," John said, his brows furrowed.

"You've convinced me," Barrett said, shrugging. "I'll probably take a few bites of fruits and vegetables. You know, to be sociable."

"Has anyone seen Ben?" John asked.

"Who's Ben?" Wayne asked.

"I mean Benji. He goes by Ben now."

"I rather like the name Benji," Barrett said. "I think it fits him. You know, more jock sounding."

"That might be the case if he were still an athlete," Virgie said. "Want us to call you Barry?"

"Forget it." Barrett let out a huff.

"So has anyone seen Ben?" John asked.

"I saw him talking to Judy Ratterman a while ago," Barrett said. "Before Ty's long-winded prayer."

"He was asking about her on the way over," John said. "I'm glad they connected."

"She had a woman with her. They appeared to be related. Maybe a sister or daughter?"

"You got me," John said. "I haven't seen her."

"Hey guys, we'd better get over to the food line or we're going to be out of luck," Virgie said, taking hold of Cindy's hand.

As they headed to the rear of the line, John noticed Sally sitting with several of the "outcasts" at a table.

"Enjoying yourself?" he asked.

"This has been nice," she said. "I've made some new friends. And it's been fun sharing some stories."

"Stories?"

"These gals have told me some things about what their husbands did back in high school. You guys were a bit on the wild side."

"I'm sure I wasn't involved in any of them."

Sally smiled. "I'll tell you about them later."

"Can I get you anything when I go through the line?"

"Some of your classmates brought ice-cream makers. I wouldn't mind a couple scoops of the strawberry when you get a chance. But go ahead and eat first. I'm in no hurry."

"Will do," John said. "Oh, one more thing. Have you seen Ben?"

"He left with two women before the prayer," she said. "I saw them walking toward the parking lot."

"Really?" John said as he stepped toward the line. "I'll go back there after I eat and see if everything's okay."

"We're just getting started and some folks are about finished," Wayne said.

"It could have been organized better," Barrett said. "There's really no excuse for it."

"I'll take what I can get," John said. "I'm usually the last in line."

"Well, I'm not."

"Why doesn't that surprise me?"

"What do mean by that?" Barrett said with an indignant stare.

"Some folks are about ready to play cornhole."

"You won't find me out there," Barrett said.

"Me either," Wayne said.

They made it through the line, surprised there was still enough food and more to feed the throng, considering that many of their classmates didn't appear to be in the best of shape, unless overly round or oval.

As they were eating, Ben and Judy, accompanied by the mystery woman, meandered on the damp path leading to the shelter. Judy's hand was on Ben's forearm as he gingerly shuffled along the way.

John was about to wave them over to the table, but Ty rose from where he was eating, walked over to them, and then led them to where he was seated.

John munched on a thick slice of watermelon before noticing Sally standing across from him, eating a bowl of ice cream.

"You didn't forget about me?" she asked, taking a small bite.

"Oh, I'm sorry," John said. "I was about to go back over and get some for you."

"You know better than that. I thought I'd wait and get some so we could eat our desserts together."

"That's good, John," Wayne said. "I'll have to remember that."

"I was serious."

"Sure, old buddy."

Twenty-three

Penny stood in front of the food tables. "I hope every classmate has enjoyed the food and the time to reconnect with friends. We have a few awards to give out and some announcements."

Those playing cornhole stopped and walked to the edge of the shelter while others bunched around Penny.

Virgie received the award for traveling the furthest distance. Sharon Dandridge was recognized for the most marriages (six). Duke Rollins received the most dangerous job award as a roofer. And Angie Lewis was singled out as the most preserved (as through cosmetic surgery). There was a round of applause and laughter as they posed for a group photo holding their dubious award certificates. Angie didn't appear pleased, facing the group with her stern but wrinkleless face.

Grover, standing near the corner of a food table, wadded a paper plate and tossed it in a trash receptacle.

"Whoever made the brownies, they were damn delicious," he said, as the award winners and others dispersed to their tables.

"I didn't see any brownies," a classmate sitting nearby said.

"Me either," another said. "Where are they?"

"Any left?" asked another. "I love brownies."

"Nope," Grover said with a smirk. "Sorry folks, someone set a plate with four pieces in front of me and I ate every single last one. You can't beat chocolate chip brownies."

With the awards session over, people went back to snapping photos with the smartphones and cameras. John walked to the cornhole area where Grover was tossing bags, waiting for the other players to return.

John inhaled deeply, pressed his lips, and strode over to Grover, who didn't notice him approaching. Grover jerked slightly when he realized John was standing next to him.

"Hey goofy," Grover said. "What in the hell do you want? Can't you see I'm busy right now? Or do you want to challenge me to a game?"

"John!" Sally shouted from the shelter. "Please don't."

John ignored her plea, keeping his eyes focused on Grover.

"I didn't appreciate how you treated my wife last night," John said in a firm, but calm, tone that appeared to unnerve his nemesis.

"I don't know what in the hell you're talking about," Grover said, tossing a bag. "I don't even remember dancing with your wife."

"Did I mention dancing?"

"Well, uh..."

"Well, in case you ever remember, I want you to know it was uncalled for, and I'm not happy about it."

Several classmates, sensing the growing tension between John and Grover, stepped outside the shelter to watch.

"Don't think you're going to scare me, Johnny boy," Grover said with an obnoxious grin. "I don't care how old we are, I'll give you an ass-whipping you won't forget. So if I were you, I'd crawl back behind your old woman's ass right now before you get hurt."

John felt his blood pressure rising and his face turning warm with anger. "Kiss my ass, Grover," he blurted.

Grover turned and faced him, eyes squinting and brows furrowed. "What did you say?"

"I said you can kiss my ass."

Grover glared at him for a second, then lunged forward. John stepped back and struck a foot behind Grover's knee, causing the old bully to fall face first in the wet grass. Stunned for a few seconds, Grover stood and made a wild swing at John, losing his balance and falling again, this time in a small mud puddle in a horse-shoe pit.

"You sonofabitch," Grover muttered as he got up and slipped back down on his rear end. John calmly stared at him with a glint in his eyes.

"That's enough," Wayne said as he walked over to John. Grover stood, wiped his muddy hands on the side of his pants, and began running toward a men's restroom a hundred yards away.

Sally came out of the shelter, teary-eyed and shaking her head. "John, why did you do that? What did it prove?"

"It proved that no one is going to dishonor you," he said. "They can do or say what they want about me, but they're not going to do that with you or those I care about."

After several deep breaths to compose himself, John smiled tenderly at Sally. Tears filled her eyes.

"I bet Grover will think twice about doing something like that again," Wayne said, smiling and patting John on the back.

"Seriously, I don't think so," John said. "Once a bully, always a bully. But I hope he'll never mess with me again."

Virgie came over, holding a beer and handed it to John. "You deserve this, buddy."

John took a quick swallow. "I sure didn't think I'd end up in something like this at the picnic. To be honest, I wish it hadn't happened. I only wanted to talk to him."

"But you whooped his ass."

"Listen, Virgie, at my age, I don't like getting into a physical altercation. Quite frankly, it's a bit embarrassing. But it was something I had to do. I know you understand."

John clutched Sally's hand and they walked back under the shelter. Several classmates came over and praised him, while others returned to whatever they were doing and acted as if nothing had happened.

"Has anyone seen Cindy?" Virgie asked, scanning around the premises. "She was here a few minutes ago."

"I thought I heard her say something about having to go to work later this evening and she needed to leave," Martha said.

"When did she say that?"

"Right before they handed out those awards."

"Gee, you would have thought she'd say goodbye or something," Virgie said, shoulders slumped and a long face. "One minute she's here, and the next minute she's gone. I guess she skipped out while I was getting my little certificate. Damn."

"Do you have her phone number?" Sally asked.

"Yeah, but I'm not sure she'd want to hear me from if she left without saying something." Virgie said. "I wonder if I said or did something to offend her."

"Maybe there was an emergency," John said.

"I guess that's possible," Virgie said with a shrug. "Everyone was focused on watching you kick Grover's sorry ass so maybe that's when she got a call."

"Seems plausible."

"If she wants to talk to me again, she has my number."

"You might want to give her the benefit of a doubt," John said.

"I'll think about it."

"When are you going back to your home, Virgie?" Wayne asked.

"I've got a flight out tomorrow afternoon."

"How about you, John? When are you and Sally heading back to Kentucky?"

"First thing in the morning."

"Maybe some of us staying in the motel should gather in the lounge later on and say our final goodbyes," Wayne said.

"Give me a time, and Sally and I will be there."

"How about eight? That should give slowpokes time to get refreshed and cleaned up."

"Sounds like a plan," Virgie said.

"Has anyone seen Grover?" John asked.

"Are you wanting to invite him?" Wayne asked, taken aback by the question.

"Hardly. I haven't seen him since he went to the men's room over there," John said, nodding toward the small building. "I hope he's okay."

"No doubt his feelings are hurt," said Barrett, who had been sitting quietly with Gloria on a bench. "You humiliated him."

"Let's not get carried away."

"Well, then you embarrassed him."

"Maybe so, but he was asking for it. Wouldn't you do the same if someone did something to Gloria?"

"He's a lot bigger than me," Barrett said. "I don't remember the last time I got into a fistfight. Maybe the sixth grade? I got a bloody nose when that happened. I'm a lover, not a fighter."

"Okay," John said, shaking his head slightly. "But I hope you get my point."

"I do have a small pistol."

"I'm not saying to kill someone."

"But I think they'd get my point if they saw me aiming it at them," Barrett said with a conceited laugh. He aimed his forefinger like a gun at John. "Bang, bang!"

"Point taken, Barrett."

"I'm going to check on Grover," Virgie said. "I'll be back in a few minutes, so don't run off. Like Cindy."

"We'll wait," Wayne said as Virgie jogged on the damp grass toward the restroom.

"I can't believe that Virgie's doing that, considering how Grover has treated him," Barrett said.

"That speaks well of Virgie," John said.

They watched as Virgie reached to the building, opened the

door, and then slammed it, holding his nose. He walked about ten feet away, waving his hand back and forth in front of his face.

"I wonder what's up with him?" John asked.

"I hope he didn't find a dead body," Barrett said.

"That's not funny."

John, Barrett, and Wayne walked toward the restroom, but stopped midway as Virgie ran up to them.

"You don't want to go any further," he said, holding up his hands.

"Is everything okay?" John asked.

"He's got the shits," Virgie said. "He's blowing crap out all over the place."

"What?" Barrett asked.

"Are you serious?" Wayne asked.

"Go and smell for yourself," Virgie said as he headed back toward the shelter. The others turned and followed him, not saying a word but unable to suppress big grins.

"Why is everyone smiling?" Sally asked as they returned to the table.

"I'll tell you about it later," John said. "It's not something to discuss after a meal."

"Oh," she said, tilting her head. "If you say so."

Penny announced that the food would be available for another thirty minutes and there was still plenty of ice cream left.

"But no brownies?" a man asked.

"I really don't know who brought the brownies, but there's not any left," a woman said. "I searched all over for them."

"They must have been delicious."

"Grover apparently thought so."

"I wouldn't mind a scoop or two of banana ice cream," John said.

"I'll go get you some and maybe another scoop of strawberry for me," Sally said. "I forgot how much I loved homemade ice cream."

While she was at the dessert table, Ben ambled over and sat next to John.

"Are you having a good time?" John asked. "Can Sally get you some ice cream?"

"I'm good, old friend," Ben said. "And I've had a great time. I'm glad you invited me. That was very considerate of you."

"I noticed you got to see Judy. Did that go well?"

"I think so," Ben said thoughtfully. "I'll tell you about it later."

Sally returned to the table with two dishes of ice cream. "Hi, Ben. I haven't seen much of you today."

"Talked to lots of good people," he said. "I had some good times with these folks a long time ago. Nice memories, for the most part."

"Some of us are going to meet for drinks later this evening," John said. "You're more than welcome to join us."

"Thanks for the invite, John, but I don't like to push it too much in my condition. I hope you understand."

"Completely."

"But I do need a favor."

"What's that?"

"I need a ride back to my place."

"Of course," John said. "I brought you here and I'll take you back home. Let me know when you're ready to leave."

"I'm not in a big hurry, but I'm getting a little tired."

John spooned a big bite of ice cream and stood. "Let's hit the road, partner."

All of the sudden, they heard someone in the parking lot yell, "What the hell!" Several men scurried out of the shelter in that direction, finding Grover next to a pickup truck, his arms going up and down like a roused rooster.

"What is it?" someone asked.

"Some asshole keyed my new truck," he said, pointing at the driver's side of the vehicle. The words read, "Eat Shit, Scumbag!"

"Who in the world would do that?" another classmate asked.

"Is John Ross still here?" Grover asked, his eyes ablaze.

"Yeah, but he's been in the shelter all the time."

Grover kicked gravel several times before opening the door. "If I find out who in the hell did this, there'll be hell to pay. I promise." He got inside, turned the ignition, and drove off, tires screeching on the pavement and scattering loose pebbles.

The men returned to the shelter and told others about what had transpired at the parking lot.

"Boy, is he pissed off," one said with a light laugh.

"Any clue who could have done it?" a man asked, glancing at those standing near him. "He accused John at first."

"Me?" John said. "I haven't left the shelter."

"That's what we told him."

"You're the probable suspect after what you did to him," Barrett said. "I'd be careful if I were you."

"I've seen several cars come in and out of the lot all day," Wayne said. "It could be anyone."

"But not me," John said.

"It couldn't have happened to a more deserving guy," Bubba said, walking up to them.

"Didn't you get into it with him last night?" someone asked.

"After he threw up all over the place," Bubba said. "But I've been here, too. I've tried to keep my distance from him. Don't think I haven't been tempted to deck him after last night. He's an ass."

"Some things never change," Wayne said.

"Amen," Ty said.

Everyone stared at Tyrone, surprised by the comment, and laughed.

"Lord forgive me, but Grover's been a bad apple for a long time," Tyrone said with a solemn expression.

"A rotten apple," Wayne said.

Several folks began clearing the food tables, loading the leftovers into boxes and plastic containers. Others started picking up litter and stuffing it into large black trash bags.

"Ready to go now?" John asked Ben. "I think we've had enough excitement for a day."

"Whenever you are," Ben said, slowly rising from the table.

Twenty-four

After helping clean the shelter, John told Sally he was going to drive Ben home, and made sure Virgie would take her back to the motel. The departure was delayed in the parking lot as classmates hugged one another and promised to stay in touch until a next reunion. More photos were taken before they got into their vehicles and drove away.

"So much for getting an early start," John said as he waited to back out of the parking space.

"Goodbyes are difficult," Ben said. "I probably won't see any of these folks again. Kinda sad."

"Same here. We all go our separate ways. But it was nice reunion after fifty years. It makes you realize how fast time flies."

"Enjoy seeing Grover?"

"That was unfortunate. Maybe I shouldn't have said anything to him. I just felt I couldn't let it pass. It was on my mind from the minute Sally told me last night."

After noticing Ben's confused look, John explained what had transpired on the dance floor between Grover and Sally.

"Any decent man would do what you did," Ben said with a hard face. "It also shows what kind of person Grover is. Unfortunately, he hasn't changed much through the years. Even Judy mentioned to me that he hit on her when she was in the tenth grade."

"I wouldn't be surprised if there were others who had to deal with his verbal attacks, even physical," John said. "Speaking of Judy, how did things go with her?"

Ben tapped a hand on his knee several times. "Uh, let me think on that for a few seconds."

"Take your time."

"Of course, like we talked about earlier, she left early in our senior year," Ben said. "I thought her dad got transferred to another city. I never heard from her after that. I assumed it was because I'm black. There wasn't much interracial dating back then. You know what I mean?"

"I really didn't see it until I was in college, and there wasn't much then."

"That's why Judy and I had to sneak around to see each other. To most people, it was taboo. It probably still is for some folks."

"So you finally got to reconnect with her today. That's great."

"John, there's more to the story."

"Oh, I'm sorry. Please go on."

"Her father wasn't transferred. They just left town. Judy was sent to an unwed mother's home in Louisville, Kentucky."

"An unwed mother's home?"

"Yes, you heard me correctly. Judy went there and had a baby. After that, she returned to her family, this time in Kansas City. She went to the University of Missouri, got married, and had three more children, two boys and a girl. Her husband died a few years ago in a small-plane accident."

"That's interesting. I guess that explains why everyone lost touch with her."

"But there's more."

"Okay."

"A year ago or so, she was contacted by a woman in Virginia who claimed to be her daughter. She had gone through adoption channels and was able to trace Judy as her birth mother."

"That's wonderful," John said. "And least I hope it was for Judy. I would imagine it would be quite a surprise after all those years. She may already forgotten about her."

"That's not the case, John. She told me she carried that with her all of her life. She always wondered what happened to the baby girl she gave up when she was barely seventeen. It tore at her, but she kept it a secret."

"I'm glad there's been some resolution for her."

"Judy hadn't planned on attending the reunion," Ben said in an even tone.

John pulled in the parking lot of Ben's condo and turned off the engine. "Then why did she?"

"Her daughter wanted to meet her birth father."

John turned and looked thoughtfully at Ben. "And you're the father?"

"That's correct," Ben said. "The woman with her is my daughter. Her name is Alice. She's married and lives in Virginia. She also has three sons."

"My goodness," John said with a broad smile. "What a wonderful story."

"As you can imagine, I'm still somewhat overwhelmed by it all." Ben's eyes began to well.

"So what are you going to do?"

"I'm going to get a good night's rest and sleep on it, then they're going to come by in the morning and we're going out for breakfast."

"There's a lot to talk about. There's a lot of history to share."

"Judy apologized for leaving like she did and not saying anything or writing to me. She said her parents told her she'd be disowned if she did. It was hard for me to understand back then, but I comprehend it now. I know it couldn't have been easy on her, being only sixteen at the time she left."

"I certainly hope everything works out," John said.

Ben sighed. "You know, life is so full of surprises, but I sure didn't expect something like this at my age."

They got out of the car and John walked Ben to the front porch. After Ben unlocked the door, they shook hands before embracing in a hug.

"Let's try to stay in touch," Ben said. "Okay?"

"You bet," John said as he walked away, turning around once and waving goodbye, thinking it would probably be the last time he saw his old friend despite the parting words.

When he got back to the motel, Sally was lying on the bed, her feet propped up on a pillow. The TV was on MSNBC but muted.

"It's weird how you can stand around all day and get tired," she said. "For some reason, I'm exhausted."

"Maybe because of the extracurricular activities," John said.

"That could be. I still can't believe you had words with Grover."

"It was something I had to do. It would have haunted me for years, right to my grave, if I hadn't said something. My only regret is that I had to do something. That was never my intention."

"A lover, not a fighter."

"Yeah, just like Barrett. I'm not sure that's a compliment." John sat on the edge bed and massaged her tight calves and feet.

"You continue that, and I'll be asleep in no time."

"Don't forget we're meeting a few folks in the lounge at eight."

"I'm not sure I'm up for it."

"Why don't you come along and have a drink, then if you get tired or bored, you can return to the room."

"I'll take you up on that."

"I bet some of the folks won't even show up. And if they do, probably won't stay long. We're not party animals like we think we used to be."

"How did things go with Ben?" she asked. "Did he have a good time?"

"You won't believe what he told me."

Sally raised up in bed and crossed her legs. "What?"

John went on to explain Ben's clandestine relationship with Judy and the reason she left Columbus. Her eyes widened when he revealed that the woman with Judy was Ben's daughter he never knew about.

"They're having breakfast in the morning to get better acquainted," he said. "They've got lots of catching up to do."

"I'm sure they do," Sally said. "That's wild."

"What would you do if something like that happened with me?"

Sally pressed her lips together. "Uh, John, there's something I should tell you about before you met me." John scooted over and pulled her into his arms.

"Touché! But, if you want an answer, it would be that the past is past, and I would forgive you."

"Forgive?"

"Forgive you for not disclosing it to me after all these years. Your life before I came around is strictly your life. Your life after me became our life. I hope that makes sense."

"I think that's fair," she said, placing fingers to her chin. "And as for you, if you told me a similar story, I think I'd be okay with it. A little hurt maybe because I didn't know about a previous love before I came into your life. But like you said, what happened before we met doesn't really count, especially if you were a kid like Ben. Teens make mistakes. It's what has happened since then."

"I can assure you that I was a good boy growing up. About the worst I ever did were those silly kissing games I played when I was a freshman or sophomore."

"It's funny, but I never played those games," she said. "I heard about them and thought they might be fun but that was about it."

"I think most of us back then were worried about getting a venereal disease. That and the evils of marijuana leading to hard stuff. And if it wasn't that, it was the possibility of a nuclear war with the Soviet Union."

"Scary times for kids to grow up."

"It's no wonder a lot of us are messed up, one way or another."

John glanced at the clock radio on the nightstand. "It's almost seven forty-five."

"I need to get a little refreshed," she said, easing off the bed. "Give me about ten minutes, and we can walk on down there."

"I need to move around a bit before I get sleepy," John said as he walked over to the dresser. "Are you hungry?"

"Not really," she said. "I don't need anything after eating two bowls of ice cream. I may have to fast for a few days."

"I'm thinking about buying an ice-cream maker when we get back home. I bet your mother would like that."

"I haven't called her since I got back from the picnic," Sally said. "Thanks for reminding me."

"I think I'm going to step outside for a few minutes and get some fresh air. Why don't you call her while I'm gone?"

"I'll do that. It shouldn't take long."

John left the room and walked down the hallway, stopping to peek in the gift shop window, and then out the front door. The sun was fading but still provided a soft light on a muggy evening. He walked to his car, double-checking to make sure he had locked the doors.

When he returned to the room, Sally was talking on the phone, or more like listening on the phone to her mother. She flashed a quick smile and held up a hand to let him know she'd be finished soon.

"Yes, Mother, we'll be leaving early in the morning and should be home before noon. We'll take care of everything. I love you too. Bye."

"Is everything okay back on the home front?" John asked.

"You don't want to know."

"Please, Sally, don't say that. You know it'll bug me the rest of the evening."

"I'll tell you after we get back from the lounge."

"I hope it's nothing serious."

"No, dear, it's nothing to worry about right now. We'll discuss it later."

Twenty-five

When they arrived at the near-empty lounge, several classmates had pushed together three tables in the corner. Sally walked over and sat next to Virgie while John stopped at the bar and ordered a beer for himself and a Coke for her.

They were laughing and glancing at him when he handed the soft drink to Sally and sat down. John glimpsed at each of them, his eyes squinted.

"What's so funny?" he asked.

"Someone told a tale on you," Virgie said.

John turned toward Sally. "Don't believe a word you hear from this group. As some say, it's fake news."

"You never told me you went skinny dipping," Sally said with a puckish grin. "I'm learning a lot about you on this trip."

"When did I allegedly go skinny dipping?" John asked, glancing at each of his classmates.

"It was in the ninth grade," Wayne said. "Four or five of us had gone on a camping trip to Deer Creek. We got bored sitting around the campfire and so we decided to do some exploring. Does that ring a bell?"

"I seem to recall that now," John shook his head with a bemused expression. "And it seems like someone dared us to strip and get in the water. Right, Barrett?"

"Are you accusing me?" Barrett said with a booming laugh.

"We must have been a sight," Wayne said. "We're lucky we didn't get snake bit or something."

"I do remember a few mosquito bites," John said.

"What about the next day?" Virgie asked. "Remember when we went down to the beach and saw those girls pointing their fingers at us and giggling?"

"Did you have to remind me?" John said. "That was probably the most embarrassing thing I had encountered at that age."

"What do you mean?" Martha asked, her head tilted.

"We'd learned a little later that they were out that night as well and spied on us," Virgie said. "Needless to say, they got an eye full. The full Monty."

"I'm glad we didn't know about it at the time," Wayne said with a light chuckle. "Has anyone been skinny dipping since then?"

Gloria raised her hand. "Barrett and I did at a nude beach in Barcelona back in the nineties."

"Really?" Martha said, eyes crinkled. "You weren't embarrassed?"

"If we had worried about being embarrassed, we'd never done it. We still get naked in the hot tub."

"Just the two of you?"

"Sometimes with others. It's not a big deal. We're just sitting there, drinking wine, and talking about everything under the moon. It's not like we're having an orgy. We're all friends."

Barrett cleared his throat. "Let me set the record straight. We haven't done it in the past ten years or so."

"We quit doing it because we weren't sure it was that healthy for us," Gloria said. "I'm surprised none of you have tried it."

"You mean taking off clothes in public?" Martha asked.

"No, I mean in front of others. I wouldn't take off my clothes in front of strangers."

"But didn't you do that in Spain?" Wayne asked.

"That was so long ago and the only time we did something like that. It was kinda fun."

"John and I skinny dipped in Colorado before the kids came along," Sally said.

"That was the coldest damn water I've ever been in," John said with a laugh. "I just about froze my, uh, rear end off."

"About the only thing I've done like that is being a model for artists," Virgie said. "They've done the same for me. More or less a study of the human body. We didn't think anything about it."

"Remember that time we climbed the water tower and spray painted 'RHS Class of '68' for the world to see?" Virgie said, elbowing John.

"You did something like that, John?' Sally asked, tipping her head. "Vandalism?"

John lightly blushed. "I confess. Virgie and I did that the night we graduated. I think it was Virgie's idea."

"Hey, you know better than that," Virgie said. "You already had the paint in your car when we went out that night."

"About the only thing I remember is that I was scared to death climbing up that ladder. I never cared for heights. I don't know where I got the idea of doing something like that."

"I'm surprised we didn't get caught or arrested," Virgie said. "The way those lights shone on the tower, we were sitting ducks for anyone who looked up. Our timing must have been right."

"Or we climbed down, and got out of there before the police arrived," John said.

"I dare you guys to do it again tonight," Barrett said. "I'll give you five hundred dollars."

"You couldn't pay me enough to be stupid like that again," John said.

"Ditto," Virgie said.

f and Roland, along with their spouses, showed up wearing golf attire and sat at the tables.

"Hey guys, I didn't see you at the picnic," Barrett said.

"We should have," Roland said. "We decided to get in another round of golf before the picnic, then it started raining about midway through. By the time we finished, the picnic was probably about over."

"You missed a nice time, especially when Johnny-boy kicked some butt," Barrett said.

"Damn. What happened?" Biff asked.

"Grover tried to get pushy with Johnny and got the shit kicked out of him."

"What brought that on?" Roland asked.

"Yeah, Johnny, why did you fight him?" Barrett asked, slanting his head in John's direction. "It certainly wasn't over cornhole."

"Uh, I hate to disappoint you, but that was it," John said, tapping his shoe against Sally's. "One thing led to another. That's all I can say."

"That was a nifty move you made on him," Wayne said.

"I learned a few defensive stances in the Army. Nothing special, but a few things I never forgot. It came in handy today."

"I'd say so."

"He did more to himself than anything I did. I just kinda let him fall on his face."

"Interesting," Roland said. "Now let me tell you about the birdie putt I rolled in the eighth hole."

"Save it for later," Wayne said.

"But you wouldn't believe it. Ask Biff here, it was something Jack Nicklaus may have done in his heyday."

"I'll ask him later," Wayne said.

"Yes, I believe we can wait on your golf game," Barrett said.

"You guys just don't appreciate good stories," Roland said with a long face.

"Speaking of stories, remember that time we went to that strip club?" Wayne said, eyes wide open as he glanced around the table. "I think it was the summer between our junior and senior year."

202

"Really?" Martha asked. "How did you get in? You were only sixteen or seventeen."

"Those places seldom carded you. All you had to do was act like you were college age. That's who they catered to."

"Yeah, and dirty old men like you," Biff said, eliciting a sneer from Wayne.

"I think you were one of the ringleaders of that carnal adventure," Barrett said, staring at Biff.

"Yep, you were leader because you were driving that night," Wayne said. "It was your idea to go."

"Sure, and you guys simply went along for the ride," Biff said with a huff. "I didn't hear any complaining when those gals shook their big titties on the stage."

"More like goggle-eyed," Barrett said, laughing. "We were speechless."

"It was just boys being boys," John said. "A coming-of-age that a lot of guys went through at that age. Kinda like sneaking through *Playboy* magazines."

"No doubt, Biff, you only got them for the interviews," Virgie said, laughing.

"Biff had quite a stash of *Playboys*," Roland said, glancing at his old friend. "I recall seeing them in your closet, behind some boxes to hide them from your parents."

"You should know," Biff said. "I had to put them back every time you came over."

Roland didn't respond, instead turned his head and took a sip from his drink.

"No doubt you had the *Playboy* magazines for the interviews," John said with a wink. "I know that's what I told my dad."

"What did he say?" Sally asked.

"He didn't say anything. He just laughed."

"You guys seemed to have a lot of fun back then," Gloria said.

"I don't remember the last time I was in a strip joint," Barrett said.

"You mean you've been in one since then?" Gloria asked. "When?"

"Like I said, I don't remember," he said. "Maybe that was the only time."

"Sure, Barrett," she said, giving him a playful nudge.

"How many times did we sneak into the drive-in to see those nudie movies?" Virgie asked. "Someone would hide on the floorboard and a couple guys would get in the trunk. Then some would climb over the fence in the rear."

"We'd also have a six-pack of beer, a half-pint of whiskey, or some of that cheap-ass wine," Wayne said. "It didn't take much to get us high."

"You were sure a horny bunch of guys," Martha said.

"At sixteen, our hormones were raging."

"Don't think we girls didn't know that," Sally said. "You were the boys our fathers warned us against."

"But you ended up marrying us because we were so irresistible," John said.

"Maybe later, after those hormones began to subside."

"We peaked at eighteen," Wayne said.

"We know," Martha said, shaking her head. "It's been all downhill for you guys."

"Now that's mean," John said with a mock sad face.

"And we improve with age," Sally said.

"I don't think I can argue that," John said, touching her hand.

"Hey, Roland," Wayne said. "Have you ever been naked in public?"

"What?" Roland said, crinkling his nose. "What kind of question is that?"

"We were discussing it before you and Biff arrived. Several of us went skinny dipping at Deer Creek."

"Well, I did streak in college with some fraternity brothers. It was more of a dare, but we had about twenty-five guys do it."

"How about you, Biff?"

"Can't say I ever did, or wanted to," Biff said. "Don't forget my dad was a minister. He would have whipped my ass if I did something like that."

"Whipped your ass?" Virgie asked.

"He wasn't one to spare the rod. He was a strict fire-and-brimstone preacher. He kept me on the straight and narrow."

"Probably the reason you were class valedictorian," Wayne said. "You weren't out there goofing off like we were."

"You've got that right, Wayne. About the only thing he allowed me to do was play golf and join academic clubs. But, bless his soul, I did get a few scholarships, and he helped me stay focused on goals. I've had a good career as an attorney, so I can't complain."

"It seems like our class had its share of overachievers," John said. "We must have received a pretty good education at good ol' Riley High."

"I'd say so," Barrett said. "We had a few underachievers, but every school has those."

Malcolm Benningfield walked up to his classmates and said, "Did you hear about Grover Jones?"

"Speaking of underachievers," Barrett said with a smirk.

"Now Barrett, that's not nice," Gloria said, pursing her mouth.

"He had a heart attack after the picnic," Malcolm said without emotion.

Barrett arched his head back. "Oh, my goodness."

"Apparently, he got involved in an altercation with another driver while going home. You know, road rage. They were cursing and shouting at each other at an intersection. I guess they created quite a scene because several people dialed nine-one-one. I heard Grover had the heart attack after he was pulled over by the cops."

"How serious?"

"I was told he was undergoing tests at one of the hospitals. There's a chance he'll have surgery tomorrow if they find severe blockages."

"That's frightening," Wayne said. "I know he was pissed at the picnic. Really red-faced."

"I hope I didn't cause it," John said.

"I don't think you caused it, but you may have started it."

"You think so?"

"He was really ticked off after he saw what someone did to his truck. He was livid when he left the parking lot."

"And don't forget his explosion in the men's room," Virgie said.

"Explosion?" Biff asked. "He set off an explosion?"

"Sorry, figure of speech. He shit all over the place."

"I'm glad now I went to the golf course."

"Maybe we can get some additional information about his condition," John said.

"I'll try to reach Cindy and see if she can help us locate him," Virgie said. "For all we know, he could be at her hospital."

"Let us know when you hear something," Wayne said.

Virgie rose from the table and walked to the lobby.

"The service around here is terrible," Biff said, glancing around the lounge. "Don't they have any waiters to take orders?"

"Skeleton crew on Sunday nights," Wayne said. "You have to go the bar to get your drinks."

"Well, that sucks."

"It is what it is."

Biff got up and headed to the bar without asking anyone if they'd like a drink. John stood and asked his classmates if they needed anything and ended up writing down their orders on a napkin. John returned with the bartender, each holding a tray of drinks along with a glass of wine for Virgie.

"Grover's at Wexner Medical Center," Virgie said to the hushed group. "He's going to have bypass surgery in the morning. He's had several heart attacks in the past, along with some angioplasties. He's also a smoker and heavy drinker, so he's not the best physical specimen."

"I hope he makes it," Wayne said, frowning. "But it doesn't sound good."

"Oh, hell, those doctors can do about anything anymore,"

Roland said. "I wouldn't worry about him. He'll be fine. He's as strong as a moose."

"And about as smart as one," Barrett said.

"How's Cindy?" John asked, turning toward Virgie.

"A little tired," Virgie said. "A long day for her."

"I'm tired as well," John said. "I hate to leave good people, but I've got a long drive tomorrow, and I need to get to bed."

"Same here," Barrett said.

"Me, too." Wayne said.

"Please finish your drinks," John said. "Don't leave on account of me."

"How much do we owe you?" Biff asked.

"It's on me."

"I'll pick up the tab at our next reunion," Barrett said.

"We'll remind you," Virgie said.

"It's been great reconnecting with so many friends," John said. "Some great times and great memories."

"You can say again," Virgie said. "Sometimes you forget how good things were back then."

"And how the bad things weren't quite as bad as they seemed at the time," Wayne said.

"Everything's changed since we were there," Biff said. "It's a shame."

"Sometimes change is good," John said. "Some call it progress."

"And some would call it liberalism. Liberals can't seem to leave good things alone."

John exhaled. "Well, guys, like I said, it's getting late and I've got a long drive tomorrow."

John, Virgie, and Sally pushed back in their seats and stood. "Good night, everybody," John said.

"Oh, I almost forgot," Sally said, holding up her camera. "Let me get a photo before we leave. Everyone squeeze together."

John and Virgie crowded into the group, everyone said "cheese," and the camera flashed.

"Hold it, let me take one more in case someone closed their eyes," Sally said, raising a hand. Another flash, and everyone eased back to their previous positions.

"Good night, everyone," John said as he, Sally, and Virgie walked toward the exit.

Twenty-six

"Why does everything turn to politics after a while?" Virgie said after they stepped out of the lounge into the empty lobby.

"Maybe he had too many drinks," John said. "I wasn't going to sit there and get into politics with him or anyone else. I came here for a reunion, not a political debate. It's not worth it and doesn't prove anything. Biff's still a friend from the past, even though I probably won't see him again. And to be honest, I really don't care to."

"I must admit it surprised me," Sally said. "Those comments always seem to come out of the blue."

"Are you guys going to eat breakfast before heading out in the morning?" Virgie asked.

"We can," John said. "Want to meet here around six-thirty or so?"

"That works," Virgie said. "I'll see you then." He shook John's hand and hugged Sally before going to his room.

John and Sally wasted little time getting out of their clothes when they reached their room. While Sally was brushing her teeth in the bathroom, the phone rang.

John had already hung up when she returned to the bedroom. "Did I hear the phone ring?"

"You wouldn't believe who it was," John said.

"Mother?"

"It was Barrett. He said that a few of them are going to the hot tub in the pool area and wanted to know if we wanted to join them."

"My goodness."

"Maybe they're going to get naked and reminisce some more about the good old days."

"You can go if you want to," Sally said.

"I think not." John chuckled as he got under the covers. "I didn't bring my swimming trunks."

"Do you need them?"

"Probably not."

"Are you going to wait for me?" she asked from the foot of the bed.

"I'm just getting the sheets warm for you."

"So considerate," she said with a laugh.

"One more thing,"

"What's that?"

"Can you turn off the lights?"

Sally pressed her lips for a moment and grinned. "I have to do everything."

Getting into bed, she snuggled up to John, resting her head on his shoulder.

"So why did Geraldine call before we left?" John asked.

"Oh, I almost forgot," she said, raising head. "She had company this afternoon."

"Brody and Ashley?"

"Frank and Dorothy."

"The Finsterwalds? What in the world are they doing in Kentucky?"

"Mother said they wanted to pay a surprise visit while in Lexington to see the horse farms."

"That's wild. I hope she handled it okay."

"She said they ended up staying the afternoon, even took her out for lunch at Olive Garden. Then they walked around Fayette Mall and bought a few souvenirs."

"Are you kidding me?"

"That's not all," Sally said. "They went on one of those scenic driving tours on Old Frankfort Pike and stopped by Keeneland."

"No way!"

"She said they had a great time."

"Unreal."

"Mother said they were going to spend the night before driving back to their home."

John raised up on his elbows. "Are you serious?"

Sally broke out laughing. "I had you going, didn't I?"

John rolled on top of her and began tickling her sides. "That was mean!"

"Seriously," she said after giggling. "They were in Kentucky and stopped by the house. Mother wouldn't tell them where we were. She was afraid they were some religious nuts."

John began to laugh. "Now that's funny. She was half right on that."

"I wonder why they didn't try to call us?"

"I haven't checked my phone for a while."

"Me either," she said.

"I had mine set on mute because I didn't want any interruptions during the reunion."

"Me, too. We'll check in the morning."

"How about in the afternoon, after we get back home? It'll give us more time to get back with them if they did call."

"Good idea."

"This sure turned into an eventful day."

"Aren't you glad you came?"

"For the most part."

"Oh, just forget that stuff with your friend, Grover."

"Would you please quit calling him my friend," John said, his brows knitted in a mock scowl.

"I didn't mean to. That's what I've been calling all your classmates."

"Not all of them were friends. We just happened to go to the same school and graduated the same year. You know, thrown in together."

"I enjoyed the day," she said.

"Why? You were a so-called outcast."

"I learned some things about you that I didn't know."

"You have to admit they weren't that important."

"I agree," she said. "But they filled in parts of your life I didn't know about."

"I lived a somewhat average life in an average neighborhood at an average high school as a teenager. There were others who had much more exciting lives than me."

"Don't you think there were some classmates who didn't do much?"

"Quite honestly, I don't have a clue. Most kids only shared with their closest friends what they were doing. I'm sure Biff didn't like Roland exposing him about his *Playboy* magazines."

"Or Biff telling the others that Roland dug them out all the time."

"It's funny thinking how risqué *Playboy* was," John said. "I don't think most people give it much thought anymore."

"Maybe it was the movies with all the 'R' releases that changed a lot of people's attitudes toward nudity."

"Probably a combination of a lot of things."

"Did you have any really close friends in high school?" Sally asked. "You and Virgie seem to have done a few things together."

"Not really. We knew each other, but ran in different circles. I really can't think of anyone, especially at the reunion. I'd have to see my yearbook again to joggle my memory."

"If you'd have to do that, then you probably didn't have any close friends."

"Hon, we're talking about fifty years ago."

"But friends remain."

"I don't deny that," he said. "But we were discussing close friends."

"You're right."

"Did you have many close friends in high school?"

"Maybe two or three, but we lost contact over the years, so I guess I'm like you."

"I guess we're two of a kind."

"I thought I would meet some of your girlfriends."

"I didn't have any steady girlfriends."

"Now John, I know better than that."

"I had friends who were girls. We were more like buddies. You know, platonic stuff. I'm sure you had boys who were like that."

"But you didn't have any steady girlfriends?"

"I hate to disappoint you, but I didn't."

"You just strung a lot of girls along?"

"Yeah, right," he said with a laugh. "You're making me out to be a Casanova. I was just plain ol' Johnny Ross."

"Was Grover really that bad of a bully in high school?" Sally asked. "I hope you noticed I didn't call him your friend."

"Thank you. And yes, he was a bully. He was bigger than most of the kids and would pick fights, push kids around, and simply aggravate students in classes like throw spitballs, put tacks on seats. Just about anything. There was a time he brought brass knuckles and another time he had a switchblade knife."

"Didn't the school do anything to him?"

"He was suspended on several occasions, but for the most part students were afraid to report him out of fear or retaliation. I'm surprised he even made it out of high school. I don't recall him ever turning in assignments. I think the administrators and teachers wanted to get him out of their hair."

"So he wasn't college material?" Sally asked with a light laugh.

"I think he joined the Marines and served in Vietnam. I heard someone say he wasn't too bad after he returned, but probably suffered from PTSD and had a drinking problem. I think he's been married multiple times. And he told me he had a construction business. That's all I know about him or care to know."

"He is *so* creepy."

"Didn't your school have a bully?"

"We did, but bullies didn't generally pick on girls like they do boys," Sally said.

"They probably abused or assaulted girls."

"I never really thought about that, but you're probably right. It carried right on through adulthood, and the cycle may have continued with their own sons in how they treated others."

"I suppose the goal is to break the cycle, one by one."

"We had our share of snooty girls who would poke fun at or belittle other girls, or even guys. And let me tell you, from my experiences as a teacher, they are still around."

"It must be that liberal education," John said with a chuckle.

"At least you can say liberals are trying to solve problems in schools instead of thinking that things were better back in the fifties and sixties, or whenever a person was in school. And I'd venture to say things may even be better than they used to be."

"I didn't mean to get you riled up," John said. "I was only repeating Biff's comment."

"I know you were."

"How about if we mosey on down to the pool and relax in the hot tub with my old friends?" John said. "It would really release a lot of tension. Don't you think?"

"I know you're not serious," Sally said, gently tapping his bare belly.

"Wouldn't it be fun to be that proverbial fly on the wall, and see what's going on?"

"Uh, no," she said.

"You're no fun."

"If you want to go down there, I'm not stopping you. And don't forget, I didn't bring any swim wear."

"That's an option," he said.

"I thought you were sleepy," she said.

"All this talk about *Playboy* magazine, sexy movies, and hot tubs has me worked up," he said. "How about you?"

"You might talk me into it," she cooed.

"Did you bring your magic lotion?"

"Yes. Did you bring your magic pills?"

"Yes, I did."

"Mine is in my cosmetic bag in the bathroom."

"Mine is in my travel bag in the bathroom."

"So, why don't you go there, and take your little blue pill and bring back my lotion. I'll be waiting for you."

"That sounds like a plan," John said as he eased out from under the sheets. "I'll be right back."

When he returned, after swallowing a little blue pill, he handed Sally the bottle of lubricant. There was enough light in the room that he could see she was already naked. He stepped out of his boxers before slipping back under the sheets.

There wasn't much small talk as they embraced each other, gently touching and kissing before they became one in rhythmic union that lasted for several minutes after which both were satisfied, and then dozed off in each other's arms.

Twenty-seven

John, his head tucked in a pillow, opened one eye at the alarm clock. It showed five-fifty. He was normally one who woke around five, if not earlier, but the sex-induced sleep had proved to be a total relaxer after a long and hectic day. He suddenly remembered that he and Sally were scheduled to meet Virgie at six-thirty for breakfast.

John glanced at Sally, who was sleeping in such a restful state that a soft smile creased her mouth. He hated to wake her, but they needed to get moving if they were going to be at the restaurant on time, and then on the road back to Kentucky.

He nudged her three times before she finally responded with a soft groan. "What do you want?"

"We need to get up and moving," he said. "It's almost six and we agreed to meet Virgie in the restaurant at six-thirty."

"Oh, honey, can you go without me?"

"I guess I can, but I thought you'd want to say goodbye as well."

"How about if you go on and I'll meet you a little later? I'd like to shower first."

John eased out of bed and headed to the bathroom, spending three minutes in the shower, and then brushing his teeth. He was dressed by six-twenty while Sally was still curled in bed.

"You must really be worn out," John said, gently tapping her foot. "I'm off to the restaurant. Want me to order anything for you?"

"I'll just have coffee when I get there," she said, her head resting on the pillow with her eyes closed. "I shouldn't be too long."

When John walked in the restaurant, he noticed Virgie and Cindy sitting at a booth by a window. She was in nursing scrubs.

"My, what a surprise," John said as he set across from them. "Did you just get off from work?"

"At six," Cindy said, her face revealing the fatigue from working a twelve-hour shift. "I'll be going straight to bed after we have breakfast."

A waiter came to their table with a carafe of coffee and wrote down their breakfast orders.

"Where's Sally?" Virgie asked.

"To be honest, we both overslept," John said. "She should be here shortly."

"Grover is scheduled to have triple bypass this morning," Virgie said. "Give me your phone number or email and I'll let you know how it goes."

John wrote down his email address and phone number on a napkin and handed it to him.

"Did you get a call last night from Barrett?" John asked.

"Nope," Virgie said. "I hope it wasn't important."

"He invited Sally and me to drop by the hot tub. The group apparently went there after cocktails."

Virgie laughed. "That would been an interesting sight to see."

"That's what I said to Sally. By the way, we declined the invitation."

"What would you have done, Cindy?" Virgie asked.

"I see naked bodies in all shapes and sizes every day," she said. "So no, I would have had no interest in spending time in the hot tub with them. Now if it were George Clooney or Brad Pitt, I would have a different answer. But I'm not holding my breath. And I'm not sure I'd like them to see my body."

"What do you plan to do after you retire?" John asked. "Didn't you say you were going to work until seventy?"

"That'll be the end of the line for me," she said. "Seriously, I haven't given much thought to life after work. All I'm trying to do is rebuild my savings and 401(k)."

"Do you have any children or grandchildren?"

"Too many," she said with a laugh. "Would you believe I have three children and around thirty grandchildren?"

"No way," Virgie said with a look of disbelief.

"I have a son who's been married five times." She giggled. "Each gal he married came with kids, and he had a child or two with each of the wives."

"Is he married now?" John asked.

"No, he's currently single but living with a gal. He told me he thinks she's the one." She closed her eyes and shook her head.

"How about you, John?"

"Sally and I have one granddaughter. Her name is Whitney. I don't think we'll have any more."

"So your son hasn't been married?"

"Brody has a girlfriend, but I'm not sure how serious it is."

"That's an interesting name," Virgie said. "How did you come up with that?"

"I know this sounds crazy, but do you remember quarterback John Brodie?"

"Sure, he played for the San Francisco 49ers back in the day."

"I was a big fan of Brodie, and when it came to giving my son a name, it was Brody Samuel Ross. The Samuel is after my dad."

"That's cool. I wish my parents had named me after a someone famous instead of Virgil."

"Maybe they named you after the old baseball player Virgil Trucks?"

"Nice try. I was named after my Uncle Virgil."

"There's nothing wrong with Virgil," Cindy said. "I think it's a strong name."

"Ya think?" Virgie said. "My Uncle Virgil was killed in World War Two."

"You should feel honored," John said. "You were named after a hero."

"I never thought of it that way, but you're right. I'm going to have folks call me Virgil instead of Virgie."

"Don't you think it's a little late for that?" Cindy asked.

"You're probably right," he said with a shrug.

Shortly after the waiter came with their breakfasts, Sally showed up at the entrance. John waved his arm to get her attention.

"I'm sorry I'm late," she said as she sat next to John. "And it's nice to see you again, Cindy."

"Cindy's told us Grover will having triple-bypass surgery this morning," John said.

"I hope all goes well," Sally said.

"Those surgeries almost seem routine anymore," Virgie said. "I know several people who've had it."

"All I know is that I don't want to have it," John said.

"I don't blame you," Cindy said. "It's serious stuff. And for patients like Grover, a smoker, a drinker, and overweight, there can be all kinds of complications."

"Did you hear about what happened to him at the picnic?" Virgie asked.

"I was there, but had to leave early. What happened?"

"He had an altercation with Johnny here, who kicked his butt," Virgie said. "Then he got the shits in the restroom. And when he left, someone keyed his brand-spanking new truck. That probably led to his road rage and the heart attack."

"I didn't realize that," Cindy said, who didn't appear surprised by the news.

"I could have sworn you were there during all of it."

"Remember, I had to leave while you were getting that award for something."

"You're right, come to think of it. You picked up your brownie tray and left."

"I do recall you walking toward the parking lot," John said. "Like Virgie said, you missed a lot."

"I remember Grover bragging about brownies," Sally said. "They must have been delicious because he ate all of them."

Cindy beamed. "That's nice to know."

"I didn't even get a brownie," Virgie said with an exaggerated pout.

"Me, either," John said.

"Well, I didn't bake that many," Cindy said. "I'm not much of a cook because I wasn't sure how many would want to eat them. I included a secret ingredient."

"You should have made more because Grover gobbled them down," Virgie said. "That secret ingredient may have been the difference."

"They weren't Alice B. Toklas brownies with marijuana?" John asked. "They were somewhat popular back in the day. I recall a Peter Sellers movie about grass-laced brownies."

"There's no grass my brownies," Cindy said. "My secret ingredient is plant-based, but that's all I can say. It's for special occasions."

"You've got me intrigued by it now," Sally said. "Maybe you can share it with me."

"Someday," Cindy said.

"So what time are you leaving, Virgil?" John asked.

"It depends," he said. "I have a few things to do while I'm here."

"I see."

"When are you going back home?"

"We had planned on leaving right after breakfast, but since we overslept, we still have to pack our things. But it shouldn't take too long before we're on the road."

Biff and Roland entered the restaurant, both dressed in golf attire. They smiled and walked over to the table.

"I didn't think we'd see you here," Roland said, glancing at John and Sally. "I thought you'd be on the road by now."

"Soon," John said. "Are you going to get in another round of golf?"

"We don't have far to travel and no timeclock to punch, so why not?"

"One of the pleasures of retirement," John said.

"Grover is going to have triple-bypass surgery this morning," Virgie said.

"That's a pity," Biff said. "I wish him well."

"We need to be going," Roland said. "Only dropped in for a carry-out coffee. It was great to see all of you this weekend. Stay in touch."

Roland and Biff walked over to the counter, waiting for a minute while the waiter prepared their drinks. They glanced back over at the table and smiled as they left.

"I think I need to be going home," Cindy said, stifling a yawn. "I don't want to fall asleep driving home."

"I can drive you," Virgil said. "We can take your car. I'll get an Uber to bring me back."

"That'd be great," she said as they eased out of the booth.

"Don't forget to give us an update on Grover," John said to Virgil. "You can text me."

"Will do," he said. "It's been great seeing you this weekend. And I'm glad I got to meet you, Sally."

"It's mutual," Sally said. "If you're ever in Kentucky, please let us know."

"I'll do that," Virgil said. "The same goes if you're in Oregon."

"Have a safe trip home," Cindy said with a tired smile.

"Next time, save some brownies for us," John said.

"I'm not sure you'd like that."

"Hey, hold it a second," John said, holding up his smartphone. "How about a pic before you guys rush off."

"I look awful," Cindy moaned.

"But still better than Virgil and me," John said, handing the phone to Sally.

Cindy stood between the men, all with strained smiles, while Sally clicked two photos of the classmates.

They hugged before Virgil and Cindy left the restaurant, leaving John and Sally alone at the booth.

"Want some more coffee?" John asked, holding the carafe.

She held out her cup. "You know, I wouldn't mind having some pancakes," she said. "Are you in a hurry to leave?"

"Checkout is eleven, so we've got plenty of time."

John suddenly slipped out of the booth and glanced out the window toward the parking lot.

"What's the matter?" Sally said.

"I'll be right back. There's something I need to do."

John hurried out of the motel to the parking and waved both arms at Virgie as he drove toward the exit. Virgie stopped and got out of the car. "What's up, Johnny?"

John ran to the rear of the car as Virgie walked over to him. "There's something I want to tell you. Grover did push you in the pool that first time. I overheard him telling a few classmates. But he said it was an accident."

"Why are you telling me now?" Virgie asked.

"I thought you deserved to know. If I told you after I found out, you might have packed your bags and left."

"You're probably right."

"I didn't see a reason for doing that. I wanted you to stay and be among old friends. I hope you understand."

"I think I do," Virgie said. "And I appreciate you telling me, even though I suspected from the start it was Grover. If it had been you who was pushed, and I knew who did it, I probably would do what you've done."

"Let's get together one of these days," John said.

Virgie grinned and gave him a hug. "Sure thing." He got back in the car and waved as he and Cindy pulled out of the highway.

Sally was eating her pancakes when John returned to the restaurant.

"What was that all about?" she asked.

"I told him about Grover pushing him in the pool."

"That was the right thing to do."

Twenty-eight

After breakfast, John and Sally returned to their room. They packed their clothes and toiletries in their luggage, taking their time, not really in a rush to get back home since they were already running late. John even brewed himself another cup of coffee and turned the TV on WSYX-TV to watch the local news and weather.

Sally phoned her mother to let her know they would be leaving in about fifteen minutes so they wouldn't get home until early afternoon. From the tone of the conversation, John guessed Geraldine wasn't too happy about the travel update.

After ending the call, Sally stood with a bemused expression. "Do you think we can spend another night?"

"Only if you get permission from your mother," John said with a chuckle.

"She thought we were on the road and that I was calling to say we were about an hour from home. Needless to say, she's not a happy camper now."

"I'll pick up the pace going home and maybe we won't hit too much traffic around Cincinnati."

"She'll be okay. I believe she's a little perturbed at Wendell and Libby. She said all they've done at home is eat and sleep."

"She should be used to that," John said. "It was that way before they moved down the street."

"Okay, honey, it looks like we're all packed," Sally said, glancing at the secured luggage on the floor. "I'm ready to leave if you are."

John finished his coffee with a big gulp and clicked off the TV. "I'm ready to blow this pop stand."

"What?" Sally crinkled her nose.

"Sorry. It's an expression from my high school days."

They grabbed their bags and headed to the checkout desk in the lobby that was beginning to get crowded. Barrett and Gloria walked up behind them, along with a bellhop pulling a cart with two oversized pieces of luggage.

"You folks sure travel lightly," Barrett said.

"We don't have to pack much for three nights," John said, noticing their luggage. "Are you guys going on an African safari?"

Barrett laughed. "Actually, we're going on to Montreal for some down time. It's one of our favorite destinations."

"We've never been there. We'll have to put it on our bucket list."

"Did you enjoy the reunion?"

"I thought it was well organized. Did you?"

"I agree, for the most part. It's nice to see people you shared time with as a kid. It may be the last time, too."

"You're right about that," John said. "It brought back a lot of memories...some I had forgotten."

"I wonder how Grover is doing?"

"He's scheduled to have open-heart surgery this morning. He may be on the table now."

"Poor guy," Barrett said, shaking his head. "I never knew him well, but I wouldn't wish that on my worst enemy."

"How was the hot tub last night?"

"It didn't last long," Gloria said. "There were a few children and their parents in the pool so there wasn't any privacy."

"And furthermore," Barrett added, "we were all tired. I think I feel asleep within a minute of my head on the pillow."

"Same with us," John said, winking at Sally.

"I want to ask you about Ben," Barrett said. "I seem to have lost track of him after we picked him up at his home."

"He had a good time at the picnic and seeing old friends. I drove him back to his place. He was tired from all the activity."

"Well, that's good to hear. Perhaps I'll check in on him the next time I'm in town."

"You might bring up some investment opportunities for him in his retirement," John said. "He could probably use some help."

"Uh, I don't think so," Barrett said with a sly grin.

John moved to the front of the counter, handing the clerk his room key. He glanced to the entrance and noticed Judy Ratterman and her daughter leaving the motel. John smiled because he knew they were probably heading to Ben's condo and then off to have breakfast with him.

Another employee came behind the desk and handed Barrett paperwork. They finished checkout at the same time.

"Until the next time, if there is one," Barrett said, extending his hand to John. "It was great to see you again and meet Sally."

John shook his hand and smiled at Gloria. "It was the same. Enjoy your trip to Canada."

"And you have a safe drive back to Kentucky."

"Thanks."

"Oh, John," Barrett said. "One more thing. Give me a call if you need some advice on retirement. You still have my card?"

John smiled and patted his rear pocket. "In my wallet."

John and Sally picked up their bags and headed toward the exit. He noticed Penny at the reunion registration table, picking up items and putting them in a box.

"Hold on a second," he said to Sally. "I want to thank Penny for putting this reunion together."

"I'll meet you at the car," Sally said as she grabbed her luggage. "Thank her for me as well. I'll start the car and turn on the air."

Penny glanced up with a tired smile as John approached the table.

"Hey, Penny, you and your group did a fantastic job putting this reunion together," John said. "Sally and I want you to know we appreciate everything you've done. We had a wonderful time."

"Thank you so much, John," she said, stepping around the table toward him. "I'm so glad you came. Maybe we'll do this in another five years if there's enough interest."

"You have my address, so let me know if you set a date."

Penny raised her arms as if to give him a hug, but pulled him close and planted a wet kiss on his mouth. "Forgive me, John, but I've wanted to do that ever since I saw you on Friday," she said with puppy-dog eyes. "Ever since the tenth grade."

John stepped back and cleared his throat, momentarily unable to think of anything to say or how to respond. Finally, he uttered, "I need to be going. Have a nice day." He picked up his luggage and left the motel, feeling a bit foolish and flustered.

He walked to SUV, loaded the luggage, and got behind the steering wheel without saying a word.

"Is something the matter?" Sally asked. "You look a little pale. Are you getting sick?"

"You wouldn't believe what just happened."

"Tell me."

"Penny gave me a big kiss, right out of the blue."

Sally let out muffled laughter. "Should I be worried?"

John gave her a questioning glance. "You aren't serious."

"Then let's go home."

The sky was a crystal-clear as they pulled out of the parking lot. John had learned from watching the local news that there had been a break in the heat wave, so it'd be cooler driving back.

"That was a quick weekend," John said as they got on Interstate 71, heading south to Cincinnati and Kentucky. "It seems like it was over right after it started. Time flies when you're having fun."

"So you had a good time?" Sally asked.

John shrugged. "Yeah, for the most part."

"Are you glad you attended?"

"Eh, for the most part."

"Now what kind of answer is that?" she asked, tilting her head.

"It's been fifty years since I've seen those people, okay? In that time, we've all grown and gone through different stages in our lives. I'd say most of us aren't the same people we were then. We share those years, but that's it. When you're sixty-seven or sixty-eight, that's a small percentage of one's life. You might even say we're familiar strangers now. I've made friends and acquaintances over the course of my life, and I would venture to say that those I've made in the recent years are more important to me now."

"I understand," she said. "My dearest friends are the ones I have now. But that's not to say I don't cherish those I made years ago."

"I still appreciate and value my classmates, or some of them," John said. "I thought one thing that was unusual, or maybe it's not after you think about it, is that those who didn't leave the neighborhood had changed the least."

"You'd know more than I would, but I can see your point. They haven't had a lot of the life experiences others have had."

"That's not to say they don't rank high on the happiness scale because they seemed content with their lives."

"Where do we fit in?"

"Hmm, let me give that some thought," John said, placing a hand to his chin. "Maybe in the middle? We're not the world travelers like some folks, or climbed the corporate ladder that some took that takes them from place to place, but we haven't been static in our lives. We've traveled to various places in Kentucky and the region, even to some distant places like Budapest."

"I think we've had a good mix."

"And hopefully more to come."

"That would be nice."

"This may sound crazy, but I wish we'd had just a little more time to say a few good-byes before we left," John said. "I wanted to say something to Wayne, Martha, Tyrone, Diane, Lenny, and a few others, but we kinda got scattered after Sunday night."

"At least you had time to share memories when you were with them. That's what counts. And you got a farewell kiss."

John shook his head. "You didn't have to remind me of that."

John's smartphone vibrated on the console. "Would you mind checking and see what that is?" John asked.

Sally looked at the phone for a moment.

"Spam call?" John asked. "Don't tell me it's the Finsterwalds."

Sally stared at the screen, then pensively at John. "Grover didn't make it through surgery."

John felt a chill run up his spine. "Damn. Would you reply to Virgie and thank him for letting us know?"

John turned on the radio, finding WGUC-FM, a light classical station in Cincinnati. Antonín Leopold Dvořák's "New World Symphony" was playing. They hardly spoke the remainder of the way, both soaking in the memories of the weekend, and the sadness of the day.

When John pulled into the driveway, Geraldine was standing behind the storm door, a wisp of a smile on her usually dour face. Whiskers' front two paws were raised against the glass, tongue out and tail wagging, ready to run to them.

As they stepped out of the SUV, John glanced down the street and noticed Wilma carrying ice water to Bert working in the yard. Next-door neighbor Manny Patel was mowing his lawn while his wife Asha was planting petunias near their porch. Rufus and Tanya Martin were washing their car in the driveway.

It was good to be back home to familiar friends.

Meet Michael Embry

Michael Embry is the author of 15 books including 11 novels, three nonfiction sportsbooks, and a short-story collection. He spent more than 30 years in the news media, working as an award-winning reporter, sportswriter, and editor for two newspapers, a national news service, and a regional magazine as well as a book editor. He is listed in *Who's Who in America*.

Embry is co-founder, along with fellow Wings' author Chris Helvey, of the Bluegrass Writers Coalition. He is a member of several environmental, human rights, animal rescue, and wildlife organizations. His interests include reading, travel, and photography. He lives in Frankfort, Ky., with his wife, Mary, and two rescue dogs, Bailey and Belle.

Other Works From The Pen Of

Michael Embry

Make Room for Family - John Ross returns from vacation to a big surprise when he is greeted by his brother- and sister-in-law, who seem to have made his house their home.

New Horizons - John Ross and his wife Sally take a long overdue vacation, traveling to Budapest for a guided tour. It turns out to be an unforgettable trip, mainly for the wrong reasons.

Darkness Beyond the Light - John Ross and his wife Sally learn their self-centered son Brody has been leading a double life and must navigate uncharted territory during the Christmas season to lead him out of the darkness of drugs.

Old Ways and New Days - Retired sports editor John Ross discovers there are many adjustments he must make in this coming-of-old-age novel.

The Bully List - Dealing with bullies isn't an easy thing to do so Josh and Sam try to come up with a list of things to do to get even with a gang of bullies.

Shooting Star - Basketball standout Jesse Christopher finds most of his challenges away from the gym as he tries to fit in as the new kid in school.

A Long Highway - A random act of violence in the workplace forces sports columnist Micah Stewart to hit the road in search of meaning to his life.

The Touch - Sports editor Blake Williams, a widower trying to raise three children, is careful to open his heart to another woman, fearful of the pain he might suffer again.

A Confidential Man - Sports columnist Chase Elliott is known as a trustworthy friend who can keep confidences. But can keeping some confidences prove to be deadly?

Foolish Is The Heart - Sports columnist Brandon Wilkes discovers there are important things going on in his life other than covering the big games.

Letter to Our Readers

Enjoy this book?

You can make a difference.

As an independent publisher, Wings ePress, Inc. does not have the financial clout of the large New York publishers. We can't afford large magazine spreads or subway posters to tell people about our quality books.

But we do have something much more effective and powerful than ads. We have a large base of loyal readers.

Honest reviews help bring the attention of new readers to our books.

If you enjoyed this book, we would appreciate it if you would spend a few minutes posting a review on the site where you purchased this book or on the Wings ePress, Inc. webpages at: https://wingsepress.com/

Thank You